The Mahabharata

The Mahabharata

Retold by Vladimír Miltner
Illustrated by Jaromír Skřivánek

TREASURE PRESS

Translated by Stephen Finn
Graphic design by Václav Konečný

Published in Great Britain in 1991 by
Treasure Press
An imprint of Reed International Books Limited
Michelin House
81 Fulham Road
London SW3 6RB

ISBN 1 85051 661 8

Printed in Czechoslovakia
1/23/04/51-01

Contents

Om!
I bow before Saraswati,
    Mistress of knowledge and wisdom,
I bow, too, to Brahma,
    Who is Vishnu and Shiva,
Who is all that is
    And all that is not.

Hear you the story
    Composed by ancient Vyasa,
A sage both honourable and holy,
    The source of all wisdom and virtue.
It is a story that men
    Will pass on, from mouth to ear,
Over the centuries and ages;
    They will never forget it,
For Vyasa's great epic
    Will achieve immortality.

Pandus and Kurus

It once happened that, during his travels through the broad lands of India, the holy man Parshara came to the very banks of the dark River Yamuna. In a boat on its waves sat the beautiful boatwoman Satyavati. Since Parshara was still young, his heart was inflamed by a glow of loving desire.

"Carry me to the island in the middle of the river," called Parshara, "and there we shall make love!"

Satyavati rowed to the bank, and Parshara stepped into the boat. When they reached the island, Satyavati said: "I am afraid, for I am still a maid, and we can be seen from both banks of the river."

Parshara smiled. "Do not be afraid," he said. "I promise that you shall stay a maid, and that no one shall see us." And, using his magic powers, he caused a thick fog to descend upon the island.

On the island that same evening, Satyavati gave birth to a baby boy, who was destined to be a wise penitent and a holy man. When he left his mother to go into the forest to meditate, he said to her: "If you need me, think of me and I shall be with you at once." Because he was born on an island, he was called Dwaipayana, the Islander, and since for the good of mankind he combined the holy writings in a single whole and wrote that great epic, the *Mahabharata*, he was given the name Vyasa, or Compiler.

King Pratipa of the house of Kuru, though he had been married for many years, still had no children. He longed to be blessed with a son, and so, leaving affairs of government to his wife and counsellors, he sought solitude on the banks of the Ganges, and did penance there. In this way he hoped to

move the mighty gods to give him at last a son who might succeed to his throne.

One day the goddess Ganga herself stepped out of the flowing waters, in the form of a beautiful young girl. She sat down on the king's right knee. The king awoke from his meditations and asked: "Who are you? What do you want of me?"

"I wish to have you as my husband," Ganga replied. "You cannot refuse me, as I have come here of my own free will."

"I cannot become your man: I am bound by a vow of penitence, and anyway I do not want a second wife."

"Am I ugly, or unclean?" Ganga demanded.

"You are beautiful and pleasing," said King Pratipa, "but you sat on my right knee, which is reserved for daughters and daughters-in-law. Wives sit on the left knee. If you wish, you may become my daughter-in-law, but you must wait until I have a son."

"Very well," Ganga agreed. "I honour you and all the Bharatas, so I will wait for your son, and will become his wife." With that she vanished.

After a long period of penitence, King Pratipa returned to his city, Hastinapura, and soon afterwards, according to the will of the eternal gods, a son was born to his wife. They called him Shantanu.

He was a bright, clever and agile youth, whose favourite sport was hunting. He often spent whole days in the forest, the mountains or riverside pastures. His bowstring twanged and his arrows whistled, as if Indra himself, king of the gods, was hunting.

One day he saw on the banks of the Ganges a beautiful girl, smiling at him. He reined in his steed and spoke to her: "Are you a goddess, a nymph, or a woman of human kind? Let me make you my wife, whoever you are!"

Ganga liked the prince's words, since she desired the same as he. "I will become your wife," she told him, "but you must never say an unkind word to me, whatever I do; otherwise I will leave you for ever." Shantanu agreed.

"Go home, then," Ganga told him, "and in a while I will come to you in Hastinapura." And so it came about.

What a grand procession it was! People speak of it to this day. Shortly before the sun set, from the north where the Ganges springs, Ganga and her companions came to the royal city of the Kurus, for her magnificent wedding. There were white and black swans, coloured fish of all shapes and sizes, and golden wild geese, carrying golden chains and golden dishes filled with amber. Flamingos held silver dishes containing blood-red corals, and cranes carried crystal trays of jasper and pearls. Behind them came the herons, who trumpeted loud fanfares. Ganga's bodyguard consisted of three troops of carp, the red, the white and the blue. A team of eight silver pike hauled a sparkling pearly shell, with a canopy made of the iridescent wings of water dragonflies, and garlanded with pink lotus blossoms, in which sat Shantanu's bride, the goddess Ganga herself. Then a great wedding was held.

Shantanu and Ganga were content in their love and lived together happily. But after a time a strange thing happened. Ganga gave birth to a son,

and she threw him into the waters of the holy river. Shantanu was horrified, but, mindful of his promise, said nothing. Ganga did the same with several other sons who were born to them, and still Shantanu was silent. But when an eighth son was born, and Ganga wished once more to throw him into the river, Shantanu cried out: "Enough! I will not allow it. I can remain silent no longer. This is terrible!"

His wife answered: "I will save this child, as it is your wish. But because you have broken your word, I can no longer stay with you. Our eight sons are *Vasus,* who were cursed to be born as humans. I have released them into the realm of the demigods, except for this last. Now I will take him with me. He shall be called Gangadatta, Gift of Ganga." Then she vanished, leaving Shantanu grieving deeply.

King Shantanu, his father having since died, was a good and just sovereign who ruled his subjects well. But he was tormented more and more by his

yearning for a son, until one day, many years later, he set off in the direction of the Ganges, without even knowing where he was going, or why. In a certain place in the middle of the stream he spotted a deep whirlpool, in which a young man stood. It was Gangadatta. The moment he saw King Shantanu he disappeared in the waters.

Shantanu was confused. He cried out: "Ganga! Give me back my son!"

At that instant the goddess Ganga emerged from the river, leading their son Gangadatta by the hand. "Here is your eighth son, Shantanu. I have brought him up with loving care. He knows the four holy *Vedas*; he is skilled in battle and a good bowman, and knows perfectly the arts of government and statesmanship. Take your son."

Shantanu took Gangadatta to Hastinapura and pronounced him his successor.

Time passed by, until one day, on the banks of the Yamuna, King Shanta-nu saw a beautiful girl with deep, dark eyes. He was captivated by her beauty.

"Who are you, and what are you doing here?" he asked.

"I am the daughter of the fishermen's chieftain, and my name is Satyavati," she replied. "I carry pilgrims across the water, so that I may bring divine favour upon my father."

Shantanu fell in love with her at first sight. He went to the chieftain of the fishermen and asked for her hand.

"She is kind and good, sir," said Satyavati's father, when he heard Shantanu's request. "I should be glad to grant your wish, but on one condition. If you fulfil it, nothing shall stand in the way of your marriage."

"Since I do not know what the condition is," the king replied, "I cannot yet give my word. I do not make blind promises."

"I wish only that you pronounce the son you will have with her to be your successor," the fishermen's chieftain told him.

"We shall see," Shantanu replied, and with a heavy heart he returned to Hastinapura. He was thinking of Gangadatta.

Gangadatta recognised that some great burden lay heavy on his father's heart, and he addressed him thus: "Father, your kingdom is flourishing, your subjects are loyal, and pay their taxes and dues without complaint; the herds are growing in size, the harvest is a rich one, and the gardens and orchards are filled with succulent fruits. What, then, is on your mind? Tell me, for I, too, am troubled by it."

Like it or not, Shantanu had to tell him all about Satyavati and the condition her father, chieftain of the fishermen, had set.

The noble Gangadatta set out at once in the company of courtiers to the home of the fishermen's chieftain, and said to him: "Listen well. I renounce my right to my father's throne. I promise that he will be succeeded by your daughter Satyavati's son."

But the fishermen's chieftain remained suspicious. "What of your descendants?" he asked. "I do not doubt your word — but who knows what they will think about the matter?"

"Then I vow to you before all these courtiers: I will never marry, and will never have children."

The fishermen's chieftain was beside himself with joy. "Then the king shall have my daughter's hand," he cried.

The gods, the heavenly nymphs and the divine holy men threw down fragrant blossoms of many colours on

Gangadatta's head, and cried: "From today the noble Gangadatta shall be called *Bhishma,* he who made a cruel vow." And from that day on no one knew Gangadatta under any name other than Bhishma.

When Shantanu heard the news, he was greatly pleased. Embracing his noble-hearted son, he told him: "I will give you a gift as well. As long as you wish to remain alive, you shall not die. Death will cut you down only when you wish it yourself." And it was indeed so in the great struggle, to which our story is progressing.

King Shantanu and his wife Satyavati lived together in happiness, and two sons were born to them: Chitrangada and Vichitravirya. When Kala, the inexorable lord of time, called Shantanu to meet his dead forefathers, the good

Bhishma gave his half-brother Chitrangada the throne, thus fulfilling the vow he had given the old fishermen's chieftain that Satyavati's son should become king in Hastinapura. But after a few years Chitrangada was killed in a battle against the King of Gandhara, who had attacked Hastinapura. Since Vichitravirya, his younger brother, was still very young, Satyavati asked Bhishma to take up the sceptre of power until he grew up.

When the first hairs appeared on Vichitravirya's upper lip, which meant that it was time for him to get married, Bhishma learned that the three beautiful daughters of the King of Varanasi were preparing for the ceremony of *swayamvara,* at which girls choose a husband from their assembled suitors.

He climbed into a light two-wheeled chariot drawn by two fine stallions, and told his charioteer: "To Varanasi!"

The place was filled with kings, princes and nobles who had gathered there in the hope of being chosen by the princesses. While the great assembly in the open space in front of the royal palace was listening as the names of the suitors were called out, Bhishma grabbed all three princesses, sat them in his chariot, and roared:

"It is said that a noble suitor who brings a great ransom will win his bride. Some exchange a herd of cows for theirs, while others simply seduce them, either in good faith or under the influence of drugs. There are eight ways of doing it, and they are all described in the laws. But heroes and sages praise the kidnapping of a bride from a gathering of kings. I therefore take these three princesses from you by force!"

The kings, princes and nobles rose to their feet ferociously, slapping their muscles like wrestlers before a match, and biting their bottom lips in anger. Their eyebrows puckered, and their eyes hurled bolts of lightning. Seizing their bows, they sent ten thousand arrows after Bhishma, but he avoided them nimbly, and sent such a hail of his own arrows against the kings, princes and nobles that each was struck by at least two of them. Soon, he was back in Hastinapura.

The three princesses from Varanasi were called Amba, Ambika and Ambalika, and Bhishma offered them to Vichitravirya as his wives. But Amba, the eldest of them, proclaimed indignantly: "In my heart I have chosen to marry the King of Saubha, and he has chosen me. At the gathering of the *swayamvara* I should not have placed the garland around the neck of any other."

Bhishma showed sympathy for her words, and sent her back to Varanasi with an escort worthy of her station. Then there was a great wedding between the young King Vichitravirya and the two sisters, Ambika and Ambalika. The girls were as brown as tempered gold, beautiful beyond measure. They had lovely hair, slim waists and rounded hips, and their breasts were like taut lotus buds. Vichitravirya spent nearly all his time with them in delights and celebrations, but after seven years he died of consumption, as suddenly as the sun sinks beneath the horizon.

The grieving Satyavati, though hurt deeply by her great sorrow, considered what was to be done for the best for the kingdom. She turned to Bhishma with these words, which she spoke from the heart: "Vichitravirya, my son and your half-brother, has died without issue. Now everything depends on you. What will become of the kingdom otherwise? Ambika and Ambalika are still young and pretty. Marry one of them, for the sake of our house!"

"Mother," replied Bhishma, prudently, "do you not remember my vow never to marry? How could I break it?"

"I know of your vow," said Satyavati, "but this is a different matter — it is to ensure that our house does not die out."

"Is there no other way? Did not a Brahman help the house of Kshatri? I am sure you know what I have in mind."

"Indeed," said Satyavati with a smile, and she thought at once of her first son, Vyasa, born on an island on the River Yamuna.

Vyasa was in his hermitage in the forest, working on the orthodox and eternal version of the holy Vedic scripts, when he suddenly felt a strange sensation. The next minute he was standing in Hastinapura in front of his mother. He greeted her respectfully, his hands clasped in front of his forehead. "Here I am, mother," he said. "What can I do for you?"

"My son," Satyavati told him gravely. "Your half-brothers Chitrangada and Vichitravirya have died without children, and Bhishma has made a vow of celibacy. The kingdom is left without an heir, and its future is threatened. Give children to my widowed daughters-in-law, so that our house may not die out."

"I will do so, mother," Vyasa agreed. But when he approached Ambika, ragged and dishevelled from his life in the depths of the forest, long-haired, unshaven, evil-smelling and unclean,

the girl closed her eyes in horror, refusing to open them until he went away.

"Will she have a son?" Satyavati asked afterwards.

"She will," replied Vyasa. "But since she would not even look at me, he will be blind."

"How can a blind king rule the land?" asked Satyavati, perturbed. "Go

now to Ambalika, and give us another king!" So Vyasa went to Ambalika. When she saw this wild man of the woods, wise, holy man though he was, with his hair matted and full of moss, his face burned by the sun, his teeth brown and his eyes frenzied, she turned pale with horror.

"Will she have a son?" Satyavati asked afterwards.

"She will," Vyasa said. "But since she grew pale, he will be pale and bloodless." And indeed it was so: Ambika gave birth to the blind Dhritarashtra and Ambalika to the pale Pandu. Queen Satyavati begged Vyasa to go to Ambika once more, but Ambika, recalling his fearful appearance, turned to cunning. She sent instead a splendidly attired girl from a lowly family, who behaved respectfully and pleasantly towards the holy man. Vyasa said to her: "You shall no longer be a vassal, and your son shall be one of the wisest

and most noble men in the land." Thus it was that Vidura was born, brother of Dhritarashtra and Pandu. He was a quiet, even-tempered young man, learned in the sciences; his nature was like that of the god of the moral order and righteousness, Dharma.

Then Vyasa went back to his forest wilderness to devote himself once more to meditation, penitence and his work on holy writ.

The good Bhishma brought up Dhritarashtra, Pandu and Vidura as if they were his own children. Dhritarashtra had great strength of mind and body, while Pandu was a skilful bowman, and Vidura was learned in all the sciences. When the three half-brothers grew up, Bhishma began to seek brides for them. The King of Hastinapura was, of course Pandu, since Dhritarashtra was blind and Vidura was of low birth.

Bhishma heard that Gandhari, daughter of the King of Subala, had been promised by the god Shiva that she would give birth to a hundred sons, and since an abundance of sons is a blessing for a family, he sent envoys to Subala to ask the girl's hand in marriage for Dhritarashtra. King Subala agreed, and soon a magnificent wedding was held. The quiet and modest Gandhari, out of respect for her blind husband, had her own eyes bound with a broad band of cloth, which she did not take off for the rest of her life.

At the same time a strange thing happened in the kingdom of Yadua. Being met unexpectedly by the divine priest Durvasas, Princess Kunti worshipped him so kindly and gently, and paid him such great homage, that the otherwise bad-tempered and irritable Durvasas told her a magic spell by means of which she could ask any of the gods for a son. The princess was curious, and at once used this spell, *mantra,* to summon the sun-god, Surya. So it came about that she gave birth to a son, Karna. He was a sturdy lad, with a strong breastplate and golden earrings. In her confusion and shame Kunti threw the child into the river, but he was saved by the charioteer Adhiratha, and he and his wife Radha brought up the boy. We shall hear a great deal about Karna later on.

Soon after this, the great ceremony of *swayamvara* was held for Princess Kunti. A great many suitors, eager to win her, gathered from all the lands around, but wide-eyed Kunti chose the broad-shouldered Pandu, sent by Bhishma, who thus showed great foresight. In this manner Princess Kunti of Yadua became Pandu's wife and Queen of Hastinapura.

But Bhishma was concerned that the house of Kuru should blossom, and so he acquired a second wife for Pandu, Madri, sister of King Shalyia of Madra. And the youngest son, Vidura, married the charming daughter of King Devaka, whose mother was of lowly birth.

One day, when King Pandu was out hunting in the forests beneath the Himalayas, he saw in a clearing a deer and a hind, showing their affection for each other. Grasping his bow, he shot five arrows at the deer. Mortally wounded, the animal cried out in a human voice: "A curse upon you! I am a Brahman and a Brahman's son. I turned myself into a deer in order to find the pleasure and diversion that the city could not offer. Since you have killed me, I place on you a curse that

you, too, will die while making love!" Then he gave up his spirit.

Pandu was grief-stricken at having killed a Brahman by mistake, and decided he would leave behind worldly things, and go into the forest to seek the salvation of his soul. He gave up his throne and all his riches, and said good bye to his relatives and friends. His two wives, Kunti and Madri, followed him devotedly. So all three left the royal city of Hastinapura and went to live in the depths of the forest.

Now the blind Dhritarashtra became King of Hastinapura.

One day, when the penitent Pandu, under the curse of the Brahman, had for some time lived the life of a hermit in the wilderness with his two wives, he said to the faithful Kunti: "Dear wife, you should have some sons. You know that no contrition, no sacrifice, libation or vow, nor any heroic deed carries the same weight in the eyes of the gods as the sons of a godfearing man. And since I am unable to have sons because of my curse, ask this of someone who is at least as good as I am. Such things have been done since time immemorial, as you know. The law says that he who owns the field owns the harvest, whoever may have planted it."

Kunti considered for a while, and said: "As a young girl I received from the holy man Durvasas a *mantra* which allows me to ask any of the gods for a son. If you think it is the right thing to do, then tell me which of the eternal gods I should ask to do this thing."

"If you have the powerful *mantra,* we shall not be left without sons," said Pandu, pleased. "Ask Dharma, god of the moral order and righteousness." So it was that when her time was up, Yud-

hishthira was born to her, and grew into an honourable and virtuous man, whose glory spread throughout the three worlds.

After that Kunti asked the wind god, Vayu, for a son, and Bhima was born, and grew into the strongest man in all the three worlds. This was clear from the start, since as a small baby he slipped from his mother's arms and fell onto a huge boulder, and he was not hurt. He did not even cry, but the boulder was crushed to dust.

At the time Dhritarashtra's wife, Gandhari, was also with child. But after more than a year the baby had not been born. When Gandhari heard that Kunti had already given birth to two sons, in anger and impatience she struck herself across the stomach. A piece of flesh the size of a two-year-old child fell from her womb. She was horrified, and would have thrown it out with the rubbish, but the wise holy

man Vyasa appeared in front of her and asked her: "What are you doing?" Gandhari knew Vyasa, since she had once offered him food and shelter when he was hungry and tired. She told him the truth, and added: "It was prophesied that I should give birth to a hundred sons, and what is this? Take the horrible thing away!"

"Do not act rashly, O queen! Have a hundred large jugs made ready, along with one smaller one, and have them filled with *ghee*," Vyasa told her. "Then sprinkle this ball of flesh with cold water from the spring. What is to be, will be." Gandhari did as she was told, and the bloody ball fell apart into a hundred larger pieces and one smaller one. Vyasa placed them in the jugs of ghee, put the lids on them, and told Gandhari to open them in two years' time. Then he vanished again, to continue his study of yoga and other secret arts in the foothills of the Himalayas.

Pandu's wife Kunti had in the meantime asked the god Indra for a son, and Arjuna was born, who was to fight evil wherever he met it, and reward the good with good deeds.

Pandu was pleased with his three sons, and he wished his wife Kunti to ask yet another of the gods for a son. But she refused, saying: "Have you forgotten what is written in the holy books? A woman who has belonged to four men is tainted, and she who has be-longed to five is like a professional concubine. Had you forgotten, my husband and master?" And she asked no more of the gods or men for a son.

The day came in Hastinapura when Queen Gandhari lifted the lid of the first of the jugs. The first and eldest of her one hundred sons was born — Duryodhana. He brayed like a donkey and howled like a jackal, and all the donkeys of the kingdom brayed and all the jackals howled, and the vultures croaked and the crows cawed. Wild winds blew hither and thither, and terrible fires broke out for no reason at all.

Vidura, when he saw these bad omens, said to King Dhritarashtra: "Your eldest son, sire, will bring misfortune and destruction to our kingdom. Cast him aside! It is written that individuals may be sacrificed for the salvation of the family, families for the salvation of the village, villages for the salvation of the kingdom, and kingdoms for the salvation of the soul." But Dhritarashtra did not cast his eldest son aside, for he loved him. And as Gandhari lifted more lids from the jugs, more sons were born to her and Dhritarashtra, until there were a hundred of them. From the small jug their daughter Duhshala was born, who later married King Jayadratha of Sindh, about whom we shall be hearing more.

At the same time King Dhritarashtra

had a son by a wife of the Vaishyu caste, and he was called Yuyutsu.

What an abundance of royal children, all of a sudden! The house of the Kurus was flourishing.

Only Pandu's second wife, Madri, still had no children. One day she went to her husband and said: "My lord and master, I wish to tell you something of importance. I do not mind if your opinion of me is a poor one. I do not mind that you consider Kunti to be better than me even though she is of a less noble family. I do not even object to the fact that Gandhari has a hundred sons. But I am truly sad to see that you have three sons by Kunti, and none by me. Kunti is my rival, so it is not right for me to ask favours of her. But if *you*

were to speak to her on my behalf, perhaps she would help me."

So Pandu persuaded Kunti to lend Madri her magic *mantra* to help her become a mother too. Reluctantly Kunti agreed, and the clever Madri at once turned to the divine twins, the Ashvini, and a beautiful pair of twins, the brothers Nakula and Sahadeva, were born to her.

But Kunti was angry, and when Pandu asked her to lend her *mantra* to Madri a second time, she snapped back at him: "She has tricked me. How was I to know she would ask both the Ashvini at once? Now she has two sons, and that is enough. I will keep the *mantra* from the priest Durvasas for myself."

Pandu's sons Yudhishthira, Bhima, Arjuna, Nakula and Sahadeva grew in size and strength, and prospered in mind and body. Soon they were known everywhere as the inseparable Pandu brothers.

But inexorable fate was awaiting its moment. One evening in spring, Pandu was walking through a grove with his wife Madri, delighting in the fresh beauty of the buds and flowers, which were covered with swarms of bumble and honey bees, intoxicated by the sweet-scented nectar. From the spreading branches they heard the plaintive voice of the black cuckoo, whose clear song contrasted pleasingly with the buzzing of the bees. The surface of a nearby lake was covered with blooming lotus flowers of different colours. When Pandu looked into the deep eyes of his wife Madri, dressed in a transparent muslin sari, desire and passion flared up inside him like a forest fire. He forgot the fateful curse, and threw his arms around her, though she struggled desperately to prevent it, and at the height of his ecstasy he died.

The grief of Pandu's two wives knew no bounds; the sorrow of his sons was beyond compare. The whole kingdom mourned the sudden departure of its king. Madri climbed onto his funeral pyre to join him, considering herself the cause of his strange death, and wishing to show her devoted love even in the next world. Kunti was left to bring up the five Pandu brothers.

When the twelve days' mourning was ended, the wise Vyasa told his mother Satyavati: "The days of glory are over. Now will come a period of decline and tribulation. It would be better if you were to leave for the solitude of the forest, and devote yourself to penitence and meditation, for in old age it is neither fitting nor good to see family bonds and ties loosened." So Satyavati, with the agreement of Bhishma, did as Vyasa suggested and, accompanied by her two daughters-in-law, Ambika and Ambalika, left Hastinapura. After spending several years in her forest re-treat she quietly departed this world.

After the death of their father, the Pandu brothers were brought up in the royal palace in Hastinapura together with their cousins, the sons of the blind king Dhritarashtra, known as the Kurus, descendants of their grandfather Kuru, even though the Pandus were also of that ilk.

The strongest of the Pandus was Bhima, who was especially an excellent runner, wrestler, archer — and trencherman; his nickname was *Vrkodar*, Wolf's Stomach. He also made use of his strength in games, though not with any evil intent, only out of youthful mischief; but it caused much ill will and envy among his cousins. He was most resented by the eldest of them, Duryodhana, who plotted how he might get rid of him.

"I'll use some ruse to drown him in the Ganges," he thought, "and I'll have Yudhishthira and Arjuna thrown into prison — then I shall be king!" And before long he put his plan into action.

One day, while the Pandus and the Kurus were holding a swimming contest, Duryodhana gave Bhima some food poisoned with a certain plant. In a while Bhima complained that he felt sick, and went to a quiet place to lie down. Soon he lost consciousness, and the treacherous Duryodhana tied him with lianas and threw him into the waters of the Ganges.

Bhima sank lower and lower, until he arrived in the underwater kingdom of snakes. There he was bitten by thousands of snakes, but their venom acted against the herbal poison he had eaten, and Bhima recovered consciousness. Bursting his bonds, he began to defend himself against attack. When he struck them, the snakes went to complain to their king, Vasuki, that a human was hurting them. But the snake Aryaka, grandfather of Kunti's father, recognised Bhima and told the snake king everything.

"Then we should apologise to him,"

decided Vasuki, "and make him gifts of gold and jewels."

"Sire," said Aryaka, "riches are not what Bhima needs. Allow him to drink of our nectar, a single cup of which contains the strength of a thousand elephants." The snake king agreed.

Bhima made the purging ceremony, sat facing the east, and in eight draughts drank the cup of snake nectar.

When he returned to Hastinapura, he told his dismayed brothers of Duryodhana's treachery, and of what had befallen him in the kingdom of the snakes.

"For the time being we will keep it a secret," decided Yudhishthira. "No one but we shall know. But we will be on our guard." The wise Vidura, who was the only one the Pandus told, was of the same opinion. The Kurus laid many other traps for the Pandus, but none of them was successful, since the Pandus were very watchful.

The villainous tricks of the hundred Kuru brothers grew more frequent, until their father Dhritarashtra decided to find them a teacher, to teach them courtesy, good manners and useful sciences. He chose the sage Kripa, an excellent scholar of all four of the *Vedas*. And Bhishma found a teacher of the martial arts, Ashwatthaman's father Drona, who, after quarrelling with the conceited King Drupada had sought

refuge in Hastinapura, settling there with his son in the house of Kripa.

Time passed by, and King Dhritarashtra, more because it was the will of his subjects than because he really wanted to, announced that his successor would be Prince Yudhishthira. Yudhishthira was very popular among the people because of his stalwart nature, his kindness, mildness, prudence, honour and truthfulness. After this decision the fame of the Pandus grew and spread even further.

This began to make Dhritarashtra uneasy. He summoned his chief counsellor, Kanika, and told him: "I do not like the way in which the Pandus' fame and glory has spread throughout the kingdom and even beyond its borders. Tell me, best of the Brahmans, what am I to do?"

"Do not be angry at what I tell you, my lord and master," said Kanika. "A king rules in many different ways. The most important thing is to hide one's weakness, as a turtle hides its head and limbs. It does not matter if now and then the king closes his eyes or stops up his ears a little, for there is no point in giving orders which cannot be enforced. And if necessary he must kill his enemies, and do so thoroughly and without mercy, even if they are his friends, teachers, sons and brothers, or even if his own father is among them. Smile, if you are angry; if you feel like laughing, put on a stern face. Act calmly, speak gently. Then strike to kill. Shed tears of sorrow and grief over your victim, and do everything that the rules of courteous mourning require. Whatever you do, do it with the future in mind, for the future is already contained in the present; the present is just the starting point."

The bent and experienced counsellor Kanika bowed, and went out. Blind King Dhritarashtra was left in deep contemplation.

The oldest of the Kurus, Duryodhana, his brother Duhshasana, the charioteer's foundling, Karna, and Shakuni, brother of Queen Gandhari, continued to plot against the Pandus and their mother, Kunti, who was also Karna's mother, although he did not know it. Though the conspirators kept their plans a close secret, the good Vidura came to know of them. One evening he went to the Pandus and told them: "You are in danger. Duryodhana and his accomplices are planning to kill you all, and King Dhritarashtra knows of it. You must leave Hastinapura at once. A boat is ready and waiting for you. Hurry!" Kunti and her sons crossed the River Ganges and made their way through the dense forest to the town of Varanavata, where they were to stay until they could decide what to do next.

Duryodhana called his spy and henchman Purochana and gave him his instructions: "The Pandus are in Varanavata and they presume I do not know about it. Go there at once and have a fine summer-house built. But take care that all the wood used for its construction is well soaked in oil, lard, butter, and above all gum, and stuff up all the cracks with inflammable resin. No one must suspect a trap! When the

summer-house is finished, declare that it is a house for receiving guests, and invite Kunti and the Pandus to stay there. Then, one night, while they are all sleeping soundly, you will set light to it." But Vidura got to know of this plan, too, and he hurried to Varanavata to warn the Pandus. Under cover of night he returned to Hastinapura.

Purochana did everything Duryodhana had told him; he got Kunti and the Pandus to move into the summer-house and gave them plenty to eat and drink.

"We must escape from here as soon as we can," suggested Arjuna.

"Not yet," Yudhishthira said. "We will pretend to have no idea what is in store for us. Duryodhana is a powerful and cunning adversary. We must make him think we have indeed burnt to death, so that we have time to prepare ourselves for his next ruse."

That evening a man experienced in digging underground tunnels came to the Pandus. "Vidura has sent me," he said. "I am to help you dig a passage out of the summer-house. Vidura said to tell you that Purochana is to set light to it on the fourteenth night of your stay." Before the fateful night a group of mendicant holy men visited the summer-house. They ate, drank, and moved on. But a woman of the wild Nishada tribe came with her five sons. They drank themselves into a stupor, and lay down to sleep, thus becoming victims of fate.

The time for flight had come. Bhima set light to the summer-house in which Purochana was sleeping and then all the Pandus and their mother, Kunti, escaped through the underground tunnel deep into the jungle.

The summer-house went up like a torch, but the Pandus were already far away, heading southwards.

They were tired and thirsty, and wanted to sleep, but the mighty Bhima took his mother in his arms and his brothers on his back, and kept on going until at last, not long before dawn, he laid them down to sleep in a clearing, himself staying awake to watch over them.

Not far from the clearing, in a tall *dammar* tree, lived the evil spirit Hidimba and his sister Hidimba. He was an ugly, indeed repulsive, fat-bellied creature, overgrown with red hair and whiskers. What is more, he ate human flesh. Smelling the presence of men close by, he turned to his sister and said: "My mouth is watering for human blood and the meat of men, still warm from the killing! Go, sister, and see who is asleep in the clearing. Today we shall have a feast; today we shall dance around human skeletons!" But when the demon's sister Hidimba saw Bhima, awake and on guard, she fell in love with him. "I must have this man with the lion's shoulders and the long arms," she thought, "this man with eyes like dark lotus flowers in a forest lake!" She changed herself into a seductive girl, and modestly approached Bhima. "Who are you, and who are your sleeping friends?" she asked. "Do you not know that the lord of this forest is the merciless demon Hidimba, my brother? But I will not betray you, since I have fallen in love with you, and want you for my own."

"If you are asking me to leave my sleeping mother and brothers on account of the delights of the senses, then I must tell you that I cannot and I will not," said Bhima, supposing that would be the end of the matter.

The demon Hidimba grew uneasy when his sister was away so long. He rushed into the clearing, and what should he see? His sister, in the guise of a beautiful girl, was talking to a human!

"Lustful whore!" he cried, and tried to strangle her.

But Bhima pushed him aside roughly. "Why do you abuse her?" he demanded. "If you wish to abuse someone, then pick on the god of love, Kama, or on me. But you shall not lay hands on a woman in my presence. I am the one you must fight!" Hidimba leapt upon him; Bhima grabbed him by the arms and pulled him away from his sleeping brothers and Kunti, like a lion dragging off his prey. Hidimba shrieked with pain, but Bhima dragged him over roots and treestumps, through thicket and thorn. Kunti was awakened by Hidimba's cries, and at once she saw the demon's sister sitting a little way off. Before she even asked, Hidimba told her:

"I am that demon's sister, and I am terribly in love with your son."

Kunti could only gasp at what was going on, and in the meantime the other brothers woke up and saw Bhima struggling with Hidimba.

"Quickly, kill him!" cried Arjuna. "Soon day will break, and at dawn and dusk demons have enormous strength. Do not spare him!" Bhima grabbed the demon, swung him round his head, and smashed him against the ground, fat stomach downwards. Then he seized him and tore him in half.

They set out again, but the girl Hidimba followed them. "Go your own way," Bhima told her, "or I will tear you apart like your brother!"

"Do not harm her," Yudhishthira rebuked him. "She is only a woman."

Hidimba bowed before Kunti: "Lady, I love your son, and I want him for my husband. Give him to me, and I promise I will return him to you."

Instead of Bhima's mother it was Yudhishthira who answered. "We can all see that you are indeed fond of him," he told her. "So take him where you will, but you must return with him by sunset."

So Hidimba took Bhima and flew away with him to the high Himalayas, where the saints and the gods sit, and there she made him happy. Then she flew with him into the deep jungle, full of sweet-scented flowers and juicy fruits, where streams babble and the lakes are grown over with lotuses, and there again she made him happy. And that very same day she bore him a son who grew at once into a young man. His name was Ghatotkacha, and he went off towards the north, saying he would return when he was needed.

Some wise holy men say that Ghatotkacha was born by the will of Indra, so that there might be one man in the world who could stand up to Karna who had once received from Indra the gift of a magic arrow.

When Bhima returned, the Pandus

and their mother, Kunti, continued their journey. They passed through the kingdoms of the Matsyas, the Panchalas and the Kichaks. They were unkempt and their hair grew long, and because their clothing was in rags they dressed in the skins of deer they caught, or made clothes of bast and soft bark. On and on they walked, until they came to the place where their forefather, Vyasa, was spending his days in meditation and the ordering of the holy *Vedas*.

"I know how badly and dishonourably you have been treated by Duryodhana," said the wise old penitent, "so I wish to give you good advice. Forget the past, and look to the future with hope. I have always tried to judge you

and Dhritarashtra's sons without bias, but now, like it or not, you have won my sympathy, because you are unjustly persecuted. Not far from here is a pleasant little town called Ekachakra. There you shall settle in secret, and no one will trouble you, for the people there are warm-hearted. I will go there to visit you." And so the Pandus and their mother Kunti found refuge in the town of Ekachakra, in the house of a certain Brahman. Their neighbours treated them kindly, and gave them everything they needed.

The King of Panchala, Drupada, nursed hatred in his bosom for his former friend, Drona. He constantly worshipped the gods, fasted, did penance and prayed that he might have a son who would kill Drona. Then, one day, when the sacrificial priest was dripping ghee into the sacred fire, a boy like a god stepped out of the flames. His head was adorned with a fine headband, and a double-edged sword glinted in his hand. In a mysterious voice he called out to the heavens: "The boy is born who shall slay Drona, by which means the glory of the Panchalas shall glow bright!"

And at the same time a girl as brown as ripe wheat stepped out from the middle of the sacrificial hearth. She had big, black eyes, long wavy hair, and was scented with the perfume of dark blue lotus flowers. They called the boy Dhrishtadyumna, and the girl Draupadi, after her father.

Soon afterwards old Vyasa, the holy sage and wise holy man, visited the Pandus in Ekachakra. The brothers greeted him with clasped hands, as is polite when receiving an honoured and old man.

Vyasa told them: "There once lived a great, wise holy man, who had a beautiful daughter, whom he had not yet allowed a husband. The girl worshipped the god Shiva, brought him sacrifices and libations, and prayed to be granted a husband possessed of all the virtues. In the end the god Shiva himself appeared to her in his kindly guise and said: 'You shall have five husbands.' 'But I only want one,' she replied. 'Did you not say to me: *Shiva, give me a husband,* five times over? Then in your next life you shall have five husbands.' And that girl has recently been reborn; she is Draupadi, daughter of King Drupada of Panchala, who is well known to you. Go there to her, and make her your wife."

Then Vyasa went back to his hermitage and, when the time was ripe, the Pandu brothers set out for Panchala. They took lodgings on the edge of the royal city of Kampilyi in the house of a poor potter, dressed as Brahmans, and took care that no one should recognise them.

At that time King Drupada announced that he would hold the ceremony of *swayamvara,* the choice of a husband, for his daughter Draupadi, and that her husband would be the one who, using a huge bow Drupada had had made for the purpose, struck a target hung from the heavens.

Kampilyi was full of merchants and tricksters, wandering jugglers and dancers, thieves, astrologers, seers, holy men and folk of all shapes and sizes. The *swayamvara* was attended by kings and princes from near and far, anxious to present themselves in the best possible light, to boast and to show off. Duryodhana and Karna came too.

The *swayamvara* began: oboes and flutes piped, horns droned, drums and tympans whirled.

Drupada's son Dhrishtadyumna took his sister Draupadi by the hand and called out: "Here is Princess Draupadi, and over there the bow and five arrows. Whoever strikes the target with all five arrows shall have the princess for his wife." The kings and princes went up to the huge bow one by one, but most of them could not even move it; only the strongest of them managed to lift it off the ground a little. Some even fell over with the effort, and rode off at once in shame.

Then Karna, the sun god's son, came forward. He easily lifted the bow, and a buzz of admiration ran through the crowd. He set the first arrow in place and drew the string. All the onlookers

froze with wonder. Then Draupadi cried out: "I will not marry a man of lowly birth!" Karna gave a bitter smile and laid the bow on the ground. The Pandus breathed a sigh of relief.

Then more suitors tried their hand. King Shishupala sank to his knees when he attempted to lift the bow, and King Jarasandha fell flat on his face. Similar disappointments were in store for Shalya of Madra, and after him the conceited Duryodhana.

Now it was the turn of Arjuna. The gathering fell silent.

Arjuna walked round the bow, deep in thought. Then he picked it up effortlessly, placed all five arrows in it at once, deftly drew back the string, and struck the centre of the target. The target swayed a little, then broke away and fell to the ground. The gathering of kings and princes roared with enthusiasm and admiration, whether or not they were pleased at the result, for the performance was a commendable one, there was no denying that. The gods, too, were pleased, and showered Arjuna with heavenly blossoms. Only Duryodhana and Karna were beside themselves with anger, though they failed to recognise Arjuna in his disguise.

A blush of modesty coloured Draupadi's face as she laid the victor's wreath on Arjuna's shoulders. Then Arjuna and Draupadi went around the whole assembly, and all those present greeted them merrily and called out honour and glory to them. Only Duryodhana and Karna glowered at them and secretly cursed.

Arjuna took his leave of King Drupada and Prince Dhrishtadyumna; he took Draupadi by the hand and introduced her to his brothers. Then they set off home together to meet his mother, Kunti, who was already growing uneasy because of their long absence.

From afar they called out: "Mother, mother, we have rare booty!"

And Kunti, without even looking out of the house, said: "Then you must share it between you!" But when she saw Draupadi, she was startled, and looked at her in surprise.

Yudhishthira thought awhile, and then said: "You were the one who won her, Arjuna, so she will be your wife. Light the sacred fire."

"No, you are the eldest; she will be your wife," Arjuna objected.

For a while they looked at each other, then at Draupadi. They sat in silence. The hearts of all five Pandu brothers had been struck by the arrows of Kama, god of love, which this tormenter of human souls fires from a bow made of sugar cane and which have honey bees for points.

Yudhishthira remembered the words of old Vyasa, and declared: "She will be the wife of all of us in common."

King Drupada still had no idea who Arjuna or his brothers were, for he had not seen through their disguise; so he sent Prince Dhrishtadyumna to follow them and to find out where they lived. The next morning the king came to them and asked: "Who are you? Gods or men? Brahmans or Kshatriyas? On this will depend the type of wedding ceremony which is to be held." Yudhishthira answered truthfully: "We are Kshatriyas, sons of the dead King Pandu." Drupada took them all off to his

royal palace, with its seven storeys, and showed all due respect to them. He gave orders for a great wedding ceremony to be prepared. But when he discovered that his daughter was to have five husbands, he was most disconcerted.

At that time the holy penitent Vyasa came to Kampilyi, and the king asked him at once if it was in accordance with the moral order for one woman to have several husbands.

"It is right that you should have your doubts, O king," the wise Vyasa replied. "For that is a rather old-fashioned type of marriage, and the Vedic texts do not give their blessing to it; but at one time it was not so unusual."

"What is moral and immoral is merely a matter of custom," said Yudhishthira. "Arjuna struck the target with five arrows; and our mother Kunti decided we should share Draupadi, which in my view is reason enough, for to obey one's mother is the first of the laws."

To these words Vyasa added: "And in the *Puranas* it is written that the virtuous Jatila married seven wise men. I myself have heard tell of the daughter of a certain hermit who had ten husbands. In any case, it is the will of Shiva, who decided that Draupadi would have five husbands."

"You have persuaded me," said Drupada in the end. "What more is there to be said, if it is the will of Shiva? Let the marriage go ahead, and we shall rejoice and make merry." So a magnificent wedding was held. The ceremony was conducted by the learned priest Dhaumya, who on the first day married Draupadi to Yudhishthira, on the second to Bhima, on the third to Arjuna, on the fourth to Nakula and on the fifth to Sahadeva. As a dowry King Drupada gave each of the bridegrooms a hundred chariots with golden banners, each drawn by four strong horses with golden harnesses, along with a hundred mighty elephants and a hundred beautiful servant girls.

And Krishna, the cousin of the three eldest Pandus, whose father was Kunti's brother, also came to the wedding, bringing jewellery, rich cloths, fine hides and lush furs, golden goblets set with precious stones, chariots with horses, a whole treasure of gold coins, and a thousand beautiful servant girls.

Let us now speak of Krishna, born as the incarnation of Vyasa in the land of Braji. For Krishna was to become Arjuna's charioteer in the great struggle, and his learning is of great value to all ages and in all parts of the world.

Braji, that pleasant land full of hills, forests and pastures on the banks of the River Yamuna, had a cruel king, Kansa. He was so evil and callous that all were terrified of him, and not even his own father was able to stand up against his will. With his cruelty and wrath Kansa wished to make up for his own fear of his enemies. He was terribly suspicious, and woe betide anyone who looked at him for more than a few moments! He would be executed at once, for the king always suspected a plot against his life.

Kansa's uncle had a beautiful daughter, Devaki, a girl with long black hair and eyes as deep as lowland pools. When she came of age and needed a husband, her father went to the king to ask his advice. Kansa suggested Vasudeva, a young man of good family.

In the royal city of Mathura a magnificent wedding ceremony was held. King Kansa gave the happy couple fifteen thousand horses, four thousand elephants, many slaves and a huge quantity of jewels and precious objects.

But there was a roar of thunder in the heavens and a terrible voice was heard from above: "Kansa, Kansa! The eighth child of Devaki and Vasudeva will be their son Krishna, who will be your doom. He will kill you, for you

are cruel and evil, and thus put an end
to your unjust rule." All were rooted
to the spot. Kansa shook with rage,
and hurled himself upon Devaki in
a savage frenzy. He grabbed her by the
hair, pulled her to the ground, and
roared:

"Does one uproot a tree, when it
flowers and bears fruit? I will kill you,
and will carry on ruling!"

Vasudeva was startled, but he knew
from the ancient books that it is wrong
to fight evil with evil, that it must be
opposed with good. He clasped his
hands, and said: "Listen to me, mighty

king! How can a ruler of your great
power be afraid of a mere woman? Let
her live, for she is your own cousin!"

"Very well — I will spare her life,"
said the king. "But you must give me
your word that every son which is born
to you will be handed over to me, so
that I may be sure the prophecy will
not be fulfilled!"

"I give you my word," said Vasudeva, sadly.

When Devaki and Vasudeva's first
son was born, they took him to King
Kansa, as had been promised. He took
the child away and killed it. And as

time went by he killed another five sons who were born to them.

The kind sage Vyasa, seeing all the injustice done by Kansa, decided that he would save Vasudeva's seventh son. From the glow of his own eyes he created a vision in the form of a woman, and said: "Fly to Mathura, where the cruel King Kansa is persecuting and murdering my people. Take from the womb of Devaki the child which is growing there, and place it in the womb of Rohini, who lives in the house of Nanda in Gokula." So it was that Rohini gave birth to the boy Balarama, about whom we shall hear more. When Devaki was to give birth to the much-feared eighth son, the king ordered his guard to put Vasudeva and Devaki in chains and to throw them into a small, dark chamber. He intended to kill the child the moment it was born, so as to rid himself of the fear which gnawed at his belly.

So, on the eighth day, half way through the Month of the Rains, Krishna was born in all his beauty, his face shining like the Moon in all her glory, his eyes like the flowers of the water-lily, and on his hands and feet the signs of divine power: a shell, a disc, a club and a lotus flower. Vasudeva and Devaki were almost beside themselves with wonder at the sight of Krishna. They clasped their hands and bowed to him, and in their hearts they feared the malevolent Kansa and his servants.

Then Krishna said in a charming voice: "Do not be afraid, for I have come into the world to inflict just punishment on all evil. But the time has not yet come, and I must go quickly to Gokula, to Nanda the shepherd and his wife Jashoda. Take me there, Vasudeva." And he turned into a howling infant.

"How can I take him," Vasudeva declared desperately, "when I am bound with chains and surrounded by sentries?" The moment he had spoken these words the chains fell from his limbs, the lock on the cell opened, and

Vasudeva walked past the sleeping sentries, carrying the basket containing Krishna in his arms. He hurried off to Gokula.

The evening before a daughter had been born to Nanda and his wife Jashoda, and when Vasudeva arrived they were all asleep. So he took the girl, placing Krishna in the cradle in her place, and went back to Mathura.

"Now Kansa may kill us if he will; Krishna is saved," he told Devaki.

Early the next morning, when the shepherd and his wife woke up, they saw the baby Krishna lying in the cradle instead of their daughter. They were pleased, because what the kind god Vyasa had promised them had been fulfilled.

Nanda at once called in an astrologer and had him make a prophecy. The man told him: "Sir, according to the stars and what is written in our books, the boy has been born in a year of good fortune, under a favourable moon, on a lucky day and at the right hour. He is a divine being incarnate, and he will destroy all demons and evil spirits, to deliver the world from their cruel dominion."

Soon afterwards Kansa heard about Krishna's refuge in Gokula, and sent demons and spirits to kill him. But it was as if Kansa's plans suited the child. He went from strength to strength, and none of the demons was able to destroy him. Months and years went by, and Kansa kept on trying to kill the child. He was always unsuccessful, and his wrath grew worse and worse.

One day old Akrura, Krishna's uncle from Mathura, came to see the child. He bowed to Krishna, and Krishna bowed to him. His uncle then greeted Nanda, Jashoda and Balarama. He told them how Kansa's cruelty had surpassed all bounds, that no one in Mathura could be sure of his life, for the king was seized with sudden rages, and gave terrible orders to his servants and henchmen. He was even said to be planning to get rid of Krishna's own father, Vasudeva. "Our beautiful capital city is groaning under the tyranny of a relentless murderer," his uncle told him. "What will become of us?"

Krishna listened to his account, and then said: "The time has come for me

to put an end to Kansa's excesses. Tomorrow, uncle, I will go to Mathura with you."

The next day a group of shepherds went with Akrura; apart from Krishna and Balarama they included Nanda, his brother Upananda, and several others. They pitched their tents outside the city walls, and Krishna and Balarama went to look round Kansa's palace. At the gates stood a group of aggressive-looking armed men. When Krishna and Balarama drew near, one of them cried out: "Be off with you, these are the gates of the royal palace! You've no business here!"

Krishna and Balarama took no notice. Thrusting the guards aside, they walked into the palace. There they hurried to the armoury, where the huge bow of the terrible god Shiva was kept. Krishna grabbed it and bent it, and the great bow snapped like a sugar cane. When King Kansa heard that fearful crack, he shook with fright, sensing that Krishna was near. But his blood-thirsty nature got the better of his fear, and he called out: "To arms! Kill! Murder! By force or by cunning — it matters not which!" All who were capable of bearing arms attacked Krishna and Balarama. It was as if a dense swarm of bees was descending on a single flower. But Krishna and Balarama soon put paid to the armed men, and walked calmly back to the shepherds' tents outside the city.

Terrified, Kansa called his counsellors and gave them the following orders: "Have the wrestling ring prepared and decorated. Then invite all courtiers, citizens, artisans and peasants, and especially those shepherds outside the gates. I challenge Krishna to a wrestling match!" Before long the wrestling ring was ready, and the first guests were arriving. The gods, too, were curious to see the match, and came soaring along through the heavens in their flying chariots. King Kansa was the last to arrive, and he sat down on the rostrum beneath a fine canopy, acting casually, though his heart was gripped by a grim foreboding.

When Krishna and Balarama came to the gate of the wrestling ring, they found a huge elephant blocking their way. The treacherous Kansa had placed it there deliberately, in order that it might kill the two brothers before they entered the ring. Krishna said to its driver: "Move your elephant over; you can see that we cannot get inside, though we have been invited."

But the driver retorted: "Move him yourself!"

"The elephant is angry, because you keep pricking him with your goad," Krishna objected, calmly.

The driver began to frown, and did as Kansa had told him he should. "Anyone can break a rotten old bow; but why don't you show your strength on my elephant?" And he gave the beast another good stab.

The elephant rushed at Balarama, but Balarama struck it such a blow with his fist that it stepped back, curled its trunk and trumpeted with pain. Realising that if the brothers were to get inside the wrestling ring, Kansa would punish him by a cruel death, the driver goaded the elephant more and more. It grabbed Krishna in its trunk and would have smashed him against the floor, but Krishna managed to slip out of the animal's pain-crazed grip at the last moment. Then one of the brothers went to the front and the other to the back, and, grabbing the elephant by its trunk and its tail, they swung it back and forth and then hurled it into the air. When it came down again, the creature did not get up. Krishna tore out its tusks, keeping one for himself and handing the other to Balarama, and they entered the ring, greeted by a roar of approval from the shepherds and citizens, and by a grim silence from King Kansa and his followers.

Then the frightened king roared, his voice quavering with terror and rage: "Beat them, kill them!"

All Kansa's wrestlers hurled themselves upon the two brothers at the same time, and a great struggle ensued. Krishna and Balarama, endowed with divine strength, slew one wrestler after another, throwing their bodies in a heap. Kansa was as pale as death.

"Soldiers! All my soldiers upon them!" he shouted, hoarsely. "Tie them up, and kill Vasudeva and Devaki and all the shepherds before their eyes, then kill them, too!"

But it was to no avail. Krishna and Balarama grabbed the elephant's tusks and, using them as lances and clubs, disposed of all of Kansa's armed men. Then a huge silence fell, filled with expectation. Krishna took a run, and with a single leap jumped up onto the podium where the once-proud King Kansa stood in his gold and crimson robes, beneath the silken canopy, a two-edged sword in his hand and a helmet on his head. But the days of his glory were gone for ever. He shivered and shook, and his face contorted with terror. He wanted to run away to save his skin, but he was ashamed of his own cowardice. He swiped at Krishna wildly, until Krishna pushed aside the other's helmet, grabbed him by the hair, and cried: "Ha, you evildoing king, you shameless tyrant! Your final hour has come! You have committed your last crime, you villain!" And he threw him down from the podium. As he fell, Kansa broke his back and smashed his skull.

Thus the most despicable tyrant who ever ruled in Braji gave up his unclean spirit.

The news of Draupadi's marriage to the five Pandus soon spread throughout the land, and Duryodhana's spies brought it to the Kurus. Duryodhana was beside himself with rage: "How is it possible? Were they not burned in Varanavata? Then they must have escaped... They have got the better of us again! They are alive and well, it seems. Fate is not on our side!"

"Do you think not?" asked the blind king, Dhritarashtra, uncertainly. "Each is the master of his own fate."

"The Pandus cause us nothing but trouble. They have always been more fortunate than we!" Duryodhana ranted. "We must turn them against each other, or make them jealous of Draupadi; somehow we must break their unity. But first of all we must get rid of Bhima, who has the strength of a whole herd of elephants."

"These are mere words, hollow words," said Karna. "Do you really think you can succeed? What did you achieve the whole time when the Pandus were here? Nothing — or nearly nothing. Now they are more virile than ever, and wiser into the bargain. They will not fall for your tricks. You must strike against them by force, destroy them; only then can you rule in peace."

"These are the words of a warrior," said Dhritarashtra, thoughtfully. "But you should hear what Bhishma, Drona and Vidura have to say." Bhishma said: "I do not like family quarrels. I honour you Dhritarashtra, as I honoured your brother Pandu, and the

sons of Kunti and Madri mean the same to me as those of Queen Gandhari. Make your peace with the Pandus, sign a treaty with them, and give them half the kingdom — they have the same right to it as you do. Keep your honour, for without it a man is as good as dead."

"These are the words I, too, wished to say," added Drona. "Share the kingdom and its government with them. Make peace with them, and send gifts to King Drupada and golden jewels to Draupadi."

"What counsel is this?" frowned Dhritarashtra. "Is this the advice our courtiers and friends give us?"

"Then why do you not admit that you have a mortal hatred for the Pandus?" asked Drona. "If what I have said is wrong, then tell me what is right!"

Vidura turned to Dhritarashtra: "Your friends have good intentions, O king, and they have your well-being at heart — you know them well enough to see that. Duryodhana, Karna and Shakuni are still young, wild, rash, and they are blinded by their hatred for the Pandus. Do not listen to them, my lord. I have already warned you once that Duryodhana will cause the downfall of your house."

"You are right, Vidura," agreed King Dhritarashtra. "The Pandus have the same right to rule in this land as my sons. Go to Kampilyi to the Pandus,

and bring them here to me with Kunti and Draupadi." This was an order which the good Vidura carried out with pleasure and without delay. The Pandus took their leave of King Drupada, and the inhabitants of Hastinapura welcomed them with cries of exultation and joy.

King Dhritarashtra received them warmly, and the Pandus paid homage to him as befitted. They also had a joyous reunion with Bhishma, Drona and the other elders of the Hastinapura court. Dhritarashtra told them: "It is time to put our relations in order. Go to Indraprastha, make it your seat, and rule from there a half of the kingdom. Thus there shall be no more reason for quarrels and squabbles between you and your cousins." The Pandus welcomed the offer, and went with Kunti and Draupadi to Indraprastha. They took with them their cousin Krishna, son of Vasudeva, for his counsel and aid.

Indraprastha was a half-deserted and neglected town in those days. But the Pandus had new houses built, several storeys high, surrounded the town with strong ramparts, and had a deep moat dug beneath them. New inhabitants started to come to the town, merchants, artisans, soldiers, and also holy men and sages. The town grew in beauty and glory; fruit trees blossomed in its orchards, innumerable birds sang there, proud peacocks strutted along its paths, and golden geese, gaily-coloured ducks and shining white swans swam on lotus-covered lakes.

And just as the River Saraswati enjoys receiving the herds of elephants which like to enter her for their water games, so the delightful Draupadi enjoyed giving pleasure to her five husbands, and they enjoyed giving pleasure to her.

One day the divine priest and sage Narada came to visit the Pandus in Indraprastha, and was received with all due honour. The brothers bowed to him with hands clasped at forehead height, and Draupadi humbly touched his sacred feet — wiping away the dust, as it has long been the custom to say. When Draupadi had left for her chambers, Narada spoke thus:

"You must do all you can to prevent any envious quarrel between the five of you on account of your having the

same wife. You surely know of the brothers Sunda and Upasunda, who sat in unison on a single throne and ruled a single kingdom, but in the end killed each other because of the beautiful nymph Tilottama." It was a wise lesson.

Afterwards Yudhishthira and his brothers decided that if any of them should surprise one of the others making love to Draupadi, he should go into voluntary exile for twelve years, and live there a life of deprivation.

Soon after that an excited Brahman, a holy man, came running into the palace to the Pandus, crying: "Robbers have taken my cattle and are driving them away! Woe is me! How can this happen in your kingdom! It is as if the crows were to peck the holy butter!"

Arjuna promised the Brahman that he would save his cows, and hurried to fetch his arms. But in the room where he kept them he found Yudhishthira with Draupadi. He stopped in his tracks, but then greeted them calmly, grabbed his weapons, and went after the robbers. He caught up with them, punished them, and returned the herd to the Brahman.

They all praised him for his deed, but Arjuna went straight to Yudhishthira: "Brother, I have done wrong, therefore I will go into exile for twelve years."

"Why?" asked Yudhishthira, surprised. "We know that what you did was necessary, indeed essential. You will go nowhere. I feel no insult; you have not offended me!"

"Brother, you have often told us that we should not avoid our duties or walk the byways of evasion. What has happened has happened. I have broken our agreement, so I will go." And Arjuna took his leave of them, and went for twelve years from Indraprastha.

He wandered through deep thickets and wild jungle, around magnificent lakes, along holy rivers; he passed through many distant lands. He reached the very source of the Ganges, and decided to settle there for some time. One day, after his morning cleansing ceremony in the Ganges, where he honoured his dead forefathers, he suddenly felt something grab him by the leg and pull him down, deeper and deeper, into some sort of underground palace. He saw that it was a small, pretty girl who had dragged him down.

"Where am I?" Arjuna asked in wonder. "And who are you?"

"You are in the palace of the snake king, Kauravyi," the girl replied. "And I am his daughter, Ulupi. I pulled you down here because I like you. Take me as your wife, for I have not had any man."

"I cannot do that, for I have promised to live without any woman for twelve years," Arjuna objected.

"That promise refers only to Draupa-di," smiled the pretty snake princess. "Love me, or I shall lose my senses!" And she looked at him in such a way that, promise or no promise, Arjuna stayed with Ulupi in the snake king's palace until morning, and in return he received a special gift: from then on no water creature could harm him.

After long travels, Arjuna reached the coast of the southern ocean, in the region of the five lakes. It was a beautiful landscape, though desolate, for no one wanted to live there. The reason was that in the five lakes there lived five fearful crocodiles, cruel and voracious monsters.

Arjuna, blessed with Ulupi's gift, took no notice of this, and jumped into one of the lakes. Right away, a crocodile grabbed him by the leg. Arjuna took hold of it and dragged it out onto the sandy shore. And, what do you suppose? The horrible crocodile turned into a lovely girl, who said in a gentle voice: "My name is Yaga, and I am a divine nymph. Once I and my four companions tried to seduce a penitent Brahman from the path of asceticism, and in his wrath he put a curse on us, making us into crocodiles. We cried crocodile tears and begged him over and over again to take pity on us; then he told us that the curse would pass only when a good man pulled us out onto the bank. So here I am." Then Arjuna released the other four divine nymphs from the spells that had been put on

them, and afterwards he travelled on until he reached Dwaraka, seat of his cousin Krishna.

Krishna greeted him kindly, and Arjuna had a pleasant stay there.

Soon afterwards the great celebration of the Yadus was held, and on that occasion Arjuna saw amid a group of girls a beautiful maiden. He could not take his eyes off her, and fell in love with her at once. Krishna saw him, and with a smile said: "Cousin, I thought you were living a life of celibacy and privation, yet I see that you have taken a liking to my sister Subhadra."

"If she is your sister," said Arjuna, "it is no wonder that she has captivated me. I should like to marry her. Tell me what I should do."

And Krishna answered prudently: "Kshatriya women choose their own men. But as for my sister, I do not suppose she herself knows what she wants, or what is good for her. Do not allow her to hesitate. Carry her off!" The two cousins, Arjuna and Krishna, at once sent a runner to Yudhishthira, to tell him what was being prepared, so that he might give his consent, for he was Arjuna's elder brother, after all.

The beautiful Subhadra was returning with her companions from a nearby hill, where they had offered a sacrifice to the gods, when Arjuna rode up in a golden chariot, grabbed her, sat her down beside him, and rode away. Her companions and guards ran into the city, calling out and making a fuss, and some Yadu noblemen, who were slightly drunk, ran out and began hunting for weapons, chariots and horses.

"Have you lost your senses?" demanded Krishna, holding them back. "What has Arjuna done which is so terrible? You know yourselves that girls do not always choose wisely. You know, too, that girls sell themselves into marriage, taking the one who offers most. And who can compare with Arjuna? Now go, and bring both of them back here." Then Arjuna spent a whole year in Dwaraka, and the rest of his twelve years' exile was spent in peace and solitude in Pushkara. After that he was at last able to return to Indraprastha.

First of all he went to bow before his eldest brother, Yudhishthira, then he hurried to Draupadi.

"Are you here already?" Draupadi greeted him goadingly, for a pang of jealousy pricked at her heart. "I thought you preferred to stay with Subhadra." But when the modestly and simply dressed Subhadra arrived, Arjuna's mother Kunti received her most warmly, and Draupadi, too, was as kind to her as if she had been her own younger sister.

When Subhadra gave birth to Arjuna's son Abhimanyu, Yudhishthira distributed to the Brahmans, the holy men and the penitents, ten thousand cows and a pile of gold pieces, to celebrate the event.

But above all Draupadi, wife of the five brothers, was a fertile mother: by Yudhishthira she gave birth to Prativendhyu, by Bhima, Shrutasoma, by Arjuna, Shrutakarman, by Nakula, Shatanika, and by Sahadeva, Shrutasena.

The high-priest Dhaumya, when the time was favourable according to the stars, and the day and the hour right, bound the sons of the Pandu brothers across the left shoulder and the right side with a sacred cord, thus making them twice-born, members of the Kshatriyan caste, and giving them full rights as members of the Pandu family.

Their seat, Indraprastha, flourished, the kingdom grew in strength, and Yudhishthira and his brothers ruled properly and justly, keeping the laws of all three forms of existence.

An Inauspicious Game

While Krishna was visiting the Pandus, his cousin and brother-in-law, Arjuna, said to him one day: "Come with me, dear Krishna, to the River Yamuna, where we will bathe and swim, and at sunset we will come back home." They sought out a suitable spot, where there was a gently sloping, grassy bank and the riverbed was sandy. It was like their childhood days; they leapt about and played in the dark waves of the Yamuna, diving and yelling.

Then they sat down on a soft and gaily embroidered blanket, chatting and gossiping about everything under the sun, except for serious matters. It was a pleasant way of spending their time, but it was soon to come to an end.

Out of nowhere a tall, brown Brahman in white clothes appeared, his hair and beard bright red, his eyes as large as lotus flowers. He gave out a strange glow. Arjuna and Krishna stood up quickly to greet him, as is fitting when such a saintly man appears.

The Brahman said in a booming voice: "I am Agni, god of fire, and I am hungry. Give me some food."

"What can we offer you, O Agni?" asked Arjuna, respectfully. "What do you like to eat?"

"I like everything which burns. I should like to eat yonder forest which belongs to Indra, but Indra always puts out my fire with his rain. You shall keep Indra at bay with your weapons, while I eat his forest."

Indra's forest caught fire, and the flames licked heavenwards. On one side stood Arjuna, on the other Krishna, and they made sure no one disturbed the god Agni. The forest burned with a fearful heat; the water in the streams, brooks and pools began to boil, and all the fish, frogs and turtles

escaped that terrible fire, which raged like the darkest of storms, and went on for fourteen days and nights: the snake man Ashvasena, the clever demon Maya, and four *sharngaka* birds.

When he had eaten his fill, Agni said to Arjuna and Krishna: "You have been a great help to me. Now I have had enough. You may ask for any wish to be fulfilled."

Krishna asked for nothing, but Arjuna said he would like the divine weapons of Indra. Agni promised he should have them when the time was ripe. Then the god vanished like an extinguished flame.

Arjuna and Krishna fell exhausted into the fresh grass by the river, and rested there, breathing heavily. Shyly, the demon Maya came up to them, bowed down low, and said: "Thanks only to you, I escaped that fearful fire. Tell me what I can do for you, and I will do as you wish at once."

"I have all I need," said Arjuna. "Only be good to mankind."

"Arjuna, I am a highly skilled craftsman, and a clever artist. You should choose something!"

"Thank you, Maya. I need nothing. But ask Krishna here if he would like something," Arjuna replied.

So Maya asked Krishna the same. Krishna thought for a moment, then said: "Maya, build me a palace such as no mortal man can build, a palace where the best of human, demonic and

died a miserable death. Bears, wolves, deer, harts, hinds, snakes, monkeys, elephants and buffalo, and the forest folk, the demons and evil spirits, all hid in vain in the thickets and caves. Parrots, parakeets and other birds tried to no avail to fly up above the blaze. They all became food for Agni, all helped to satiate his hunger. Only six creatures divine building arts shall be combined."

"Very well, Krishna, I will build you such a palace; and there shall be none like it in any of the three worlds," Maya promised, and he set to work at once. In fourteen months he and his helpers had built such a magnificent palace that none of the gods had one more beautiful or more imposing. And when the palace was completed, and lotus lakes had been made around it, with ornamental fish and water fowl, and pleasant groves and orchards had been planted, Krishna gave the palace and all that belonged to it to Yudhishthira, so that he could rule his kingdom from it.

To celebrate the event King Yudhishthira held a feast for a thousand Brahmans, and gave them rice pudding with butter and honey, many kinds of well-roasted meat with spiced sauce, and various fruits and yogurt. He also gave the saintly men gifts of rare clothes, floral garlands and herds of cows. The Brahmans praised and honoured him so loudly that even the gods in heaven and the hermits, wise men and penitents for many a mile, heard them. Among those who heard was the wise saint and holy sage Narada, versed in the laws and in logic, phonetics, grammar, poetry, etymology, ceremonies and sacrifices, astronomy, music, the martial arts and warfare, and he came to Yudhishthira to teach him

about the matters which every good ruler should know. There were many such things; then, when he had finished, the wise Narada said: "But remember, Yudhishthira, that even the best of kings may destroy himself." Then he left, accompanied by the saints and wise men who were there.

Yudhishthira ruled well and justly. The four branches of the economy, that is agriculture, crafts and trade, the rearing of animals and monetary matters were controlled by honourable and trustworthy men. As far as his subjects were concerned, Yudhishthira stuck to the principle of each according to his merits and needs. And all his subjects worked according to their abilities. It was a happy kingdom.

"I have been thinking for some time," said Yudhishthira to Krishna one day, when they were alone, "of making the great royal sacrifice of *Rajasuya*. But as you know, there is a chasm of effort and time between the idea and its realisation. My counsellors and friends are in favour of it, but friends do not usually see all the difficulties involved, and counsellors are anxious to please. So I should like to know your opinion of the matter, Krishna, and to ask your advice."

Krishna replied gravely: "You deserve your honour as a ruler to be confirmed and strengthened by the great royal sacrifice, but King Jarasandha of

Magadha is still opposed to you; surely you have not forgotten that time when I had to flee from his lackeys in Mathura. So I would advise you thus: first of all destroy Jarasandha and deliver the kings he holds captive. Only then should you hold the *Rajasuya*."

"You are right," said Yudhishthira, "but how am I to stand up to a king as strong as he?"

Bhima, who had just entered together with Arjuna, heard the last words, and interjected: "Why not, brother? We will help you — Krishna is wise, Arjuna courageous, and I am strong."

"We must think the matter over carefully," said Krishna, emphatically. "Jarasandha is truly strong. Has he not defeated and imprisoned eighty kings, whom he holds prisoner in the underground chambers of Shiva's temple? When he has a hundred of them, he wants to have them all executed, and to hold the great sacrifice of kings for himself. We must not move too soon, but we must not waste time, either." So they put their heads together and decided how they should tackle King Jarasandha. And they carried out their plans the very next day.

Krishna, Arjuna and Bhima dressed up as mendicant holy men and set out for Magadha. Jarasandha's royal city was indeed rich and imposing. The market was filled with all kinds of goods, including the rare and the precious. There Krishna, Arjuna and Bhima decorated themselves with garlands of flowers around their necks, and set out boldly for the royal palace.

King Jarasandha came to meet them. "Welcome, holy men!" he cried, and at once he gave them a herd of cows as a gift.

Arjuna and Bhima were silent, and Krishna explained to the king: "My companions have to keep a vow of silence until midnight. Then they will speak to you." Jarasandha had the false holy men shown into a luxurious chamber, and came to visit them after midnight. He greeted them and sat down.

"Soon, O king," Krishna said to him, and looked meaningfully at his brothers, "you will achieve eternal salvation." And the king asked: "Who are you? I have never seen holy men with the manners of Kshatriyas."

"We behave in that manner," Krishna told him, "because we consider you our enemy."

"But why? I have not harmed you. You do me wrong."

"Then what of the eighty kings you hold prisoner in the temple of Shiva? We have come to kill you. I am Krishna, and these men are Arjuna and Bhima. We challenge you to a wrestling match. Either you release all the kings you hold prisoner, or you will die."

"I captured those kings in battle, and have promised them as a sacrifice to Shiva!" cried Jarasandha, angrily. "And your threats do not frighten me! Come, then, we will fight!"

"Choose which of us will be the first," Krishna said. Jarasandha chose Bhima, and that sealed his fate. He took off his royal crown, tied back his hair, and took up the starting position.

"I chose you, Bhima, because if you win, I will die happy, having been defeated by a better man than myself." And they threw themselves upon each other.

The match was a short, but cruel

one. Bhima lifted Jarasandha up high, swung him round, and then brought him down onto the ground. He knelt on the king's chest with his right knee, grabbed him by the legs, and tore him in half. King Jarasandha gave a fearful cry, a cry of pain, and Bhima also gave a fearful cry, but his was of victory. That double cry filled the whole of Magadha with terror; people were afraid that the Himalayas were collapsing; many old people died of fright, and many children came into the world before their time.

Krishna ran to the temple of Shiva to release the kings held prisoner there, and these became allies of Yudhishthira; then he and Arjuna and Bhima hurried back to Indraprastha.

Arjuna announced to Yudhishthira: "We have arms, soldiers, allies. Now the only thing left to do is to fill the royal coffers." So they set out to win booty. Bhima went eastwards, Sahadeva southwards, Nakula westwards and Arjuna northwards. They subdued many a kingdom, whose kings took oaths of alliance and fealty, and with gifts, ransoms and martial honour they returned home.

"Now is the time to hold the great royal sacrificial ceremony," Krishna declared. All the friendly and allied kings were invited, along with thousands of Brahmans, holy men and penitents, and, of course, King Dhritarashtra along with Queen Gandhari and all their sons and their one daughter.

When all the guests came together at the great gathering around the holy fire, good Bhishma stood up and proclaimed ceremoniously:

"To begin with, let us honour the noble Krishna, whose presence among us is like the sunshine in darkness, and like a breeze in the airlessness of space." At this King Shishupala spoke up disdainfully: "Why should Krishna be the one to be honoured? Is there no one here who is better, more worthy of honour? What of King Dhritarashtra, the teacher Drona, or the holy Vyasa? Krishna is neither king, nor teacher, nor holy man. What did he give you, Bhishma, for putting forward his name?" And he rose, and made as if to leave the gathering.

Yudhishthira went over to him and said: "You have spoken foolishly, Shishupala; not only that, but you have greatly insulted Bhishma."

"There is no point in talking to someone who does not understand why we honour Krishna," said Bhishma, calmly. "Krishna is modest, wise, honourable, valiant and just, and with his divine might maintains order and regularity in the world."

Then Sahadeva spoke: "If there is a king among you so proud that he does not wish to honour the noble Krishna, let him speak out, and I will stamp on his head." And he looked around him belligerently.

A hum ran round the gathering as if from a beehive. Some agreed, while others were against.

Shishupala cried out: "Why are we here, anyway? Let us beat them!"

Though the ceremony continued, the confusion spread among the throng. Bhishma said to the anxious Yudhishthira: "Keep calm! The dogs bark at a lion, but the lion ignores them."

Shishupala shouted until he was hoarse: "You stupid old man, Bhishma, do you think you can threaten us? You old woman, who has not even been able to have a son! Is this celibacy, or is it impotence? Only the foolish can honour Krishna, before whom women and herds of cows are unsure of themselves! Before that Krishna who dressed as a holy man, in order to go with Arjuna and Bhima treacherously to slay King Jarasandha!"

Three veins stood out on Bhima's forehead, so angry was he, like the three tributaries of the Ganges; he grit-

ted his teeth, and he would have leapt upon Shishupala, but Bhishma held him back.

"Let him go, Bhishma," Shishupala went on goading them. "Let him go — he will burn up like a moth in the flame of my strength! And you, Krishna, I hold in disdain, too!"

Krishna stood up and addressed the gathering: "Shishupala is the son of my father's sister. He looted and laid waste the city of Dwaraka; he deflowered the wife of my uncle, Akrura, and Princess Bhadra of Ujjayina. All that I put up with. He committed many crimes and did many wrongs, but I bore all of it with patience, since he is the son of my father's sister. I have forgiven him a hundred times; but today, on the hundred and first occasion, I will forgive him no more."

He took his heavenly discus, threw it at Shishupala, and cut off his head. Shishupala was toppled like a tree struck by lightning. The gathering fell silent; servants carried off the body, and the great sacrifice of kings, the *Rajasuya,* continued, and came to a successful conclusion.

When the *Rajasuya* was over, the holy sage Vyasa came up to Yudhishthira, embraced him, and said: "I am pleased at your success, Yudhishthira! You have done the right thing."

All the guests left except for the Kurus and their uncle, Shakuni, who stayed a few more days. Duryodhana was very jealous of the honour shown to Yudhishthira because of his success in holding the great sacrifice of kings, but he was even more envious of his magnificent palace, the finest work of the skilful demon Maya. Together with Shakuni he went through different levels with all their rooms, staircases, passages and alcoves, and climbed all the towers and nosed around in all the cellars; but if anyone had asked him, he would not even have been able to describe it properly.

Once he banged his head on a closed door made of crystal, because he thought it was open; other doors he tried to force, when they were wide open already. He cursed quietly, turned pale with anger, and was ashamed of his stupidity.

He thought a crystal floor was a swimming-pool, and lifted his robes so as not to wet them. Then he thought he was stepping onto a crystal floor, but fell into a swimming-pool and had to go and change his clothes. Arjuna only laughed at him a little, but Bhima laughed his head off. Duryodhana bowed his head in shame, and inside he was seized with a helpless anger. Quite put out, he took his brothers and his uncle Shakuni, and returned to Hastinapura filled with envy of his cousins, the Pandus.

The malevolent Shakuni noticed this. He sidled up to the king, and, though everything was clear to him, asked ob-

sequiously: "What is the matter? You look as if something was worrying you. You are going about like a man in a dream, swearing to yourself, frowning and scowling."

"Are you surprised?" snapped Duryodhana, pouring out his pent-up wrath. "No one stood up for Shishupala when Krishna killed him. They all let themselves be cowed. Yudhishthira has subjugated hundreds of kings, who now bow to his sovereignty and pay taxes to him. And the Pandus succeed in all things. I envy them and hate them. I know it is wrong, but I cannot help it. I have a great fire burning inside me, and do not know what to do. As long as the Pandus succeed in everything they turn their hands to, life will have no meaning for me. They laughed at me with every step I took in their palace; they giggled at me! The humiliation of it . . ."

"They are stalwart warriors, there is no denying that," said Shakuni, cunningly, "so it would be best to avoid meeting them in open battle. But I might know a way . . ."

"Speak out," Duryodhana interrupted. "Speak — quickly!"

"Yudhishthira has a weakness for the game of backgammon, and he is not a good player. If I challenge him to a game, he is sure to accept. Then I am able to win everything! But first of all I must ask King Dhritarashtra for permission."

Duryodhana did not delay. He put his arm round Shakuni's shoulders and set off to Dhritarashtra with him.

They greeted the blind king, and when he asked what brought them, Shakuni told him straight out: "My lord and brother-in-law, Duryodhana is sad and troubled by grim thoughts. Ask him for yourself, so that you may know all."

"What is it, my son?" Dhritarashtra asked. "What weight is on your mind? Why are you so out of spirit? Were you not pleased with the magnificent rooms, the tasty foods, the good drink and the willing paramours in Yudhishthira's luxurious palace?"

"That is the very thing which makes me so angry, Father," Duryodhana replied, unhappily. "The success of the Pandus is my downfall. Yudhishthira in particular makes me see red. He gave thirty slave-girls each to eighty-eight Brahmans. He entertains thousands of holy men to fine delicacies served on golden dishes. The ceremonial sound of shells being blown is heard there all day long; the kings from the surrounding kingdoms visit him in droves, and each of them takes gifts away with him. I cannot stand it! Father, Shakuni is an excellent backgammon player. Allow him to challenge Yudhishthira to a game!"

"In such a serious matter I must take the advice of my counsellor, Vidura," King Dhritarashtra replied. "I will

tell you of my decision afterwards."
"No, father, please," blurted out
Duryodhana. "Vidura would surely be
against it. Father, I am terribly unhappy. Almost at the point of suicide."

"Very well, then," the old and
weak Dhritarashtra agreed. "Tell our
builders to build a fine gaming room
with a hundred doors and a thousand
columns." When he had said this, he at
once called in Vidura, whose counsel
he valued dearly.

Vidura thought awhile, then said:
"I am afraid, my lord and master, that
this is not a good idea; I would even

say it was a very bad idea, an unwise one. A game of dice has never yet made friends of enemies. Quite the opposite."

"But Vidura," King Dhritarashtra soothed him. "A game is just a game! If the gods are favourably inclined, all will turn out well. You and I will be present, after all, and Drona, and Bhishma. Take a chariot and go to Indraprastha to invite Yudhishthira and the other Pandus, along with Kunti and Draupadi, to visit us in Hastinapura. Fate is fate."

So Vidura, like it or not, and grumbling in spirit, rode to Indraprastha.

None the less, Dhritarashtra had words with Duryodhana. "You are the eldest of my sons by my first wife, Gandhari. I should not like you to do anything which was not in accordance with the moral order," he told him clearly. "Remember that everything in this world must be paid for with the tax of justice. Do not sow evil, for you must answer for all your deeds."

But Duryodhana took no notice of his father's warning words, and was eager to have his own way.

When Vidura reached Indraprastha and was greeted by Yudhishthira and the other Pandus, Yudhishthira commented at once: "What has happened, honourable Vidura, that you look so worried? Has some misfortune occurred in Hastinapura?"

"It has not, and yet it has, my dear Yudhishthira," replied the good Vidura. "The king is healthy and contented, but he sends me to invite you to play backgammon."

Yudhishthira nodded his head and said: "Games of chance give rise to quarrels, fighting and hatred. I do not want to go there."

"My feeling is the same," Vidura replied. "But do not forget that I bring you the invitation of Dhritarashtra."

"Hm. Then I cannot refuse. Who is to play against me?"

"Shakuni, King of Gandhara, who always plays for high stakes," Vidura told him. "And perhaps others, too. I do not know."

"Then my chances are indeed poor," sighed Yudhishthira. "But I do not refuse the invitation." And he rode to Hastinapura.

When the Pandus had arrived in Hastinapura and paid their respects to the blind old king and to Queen Gandhari, Dhritarashtra welcomed them according to age-old custom. He entertained them lavishly, and since it was evening, had them taken to their chambers, where lovely girls sang them to sleep.

In the morning the Pandus entered the great gaming room, where the Kurus and some of Dhritarashtra's subject kings were waiting. The last to arrive was Duryodhana, accompanied by Vidura, Bhishma, Drona and Kripa.

"Now we are all here," declared Shakuni, anxious for the game to start. "So we can begin."

"Games of chance are not a good thing," said Yudhishthira. "They are not games for Kshatriyas. Why do you attack us with such a dubious weapon, Shakuni?"

"A game is like a battle," replied Shakuni. "The best man wins. The desire to bring one's enemy to nought is always a dubious one, whether in a game, a fight, or a debate between wise men. But if you are afraid of losing, there is still time to withdraw."

"Whether I am challenged to a game, a fight or a debate, I never refuse," Yudhishthira said. "Then let us start. Who is to play against me?"

Duryodhana quickly replied: "I will wager, and my Uncle Shakuni will play."

"That is not according to the rules," objected Yudhishthira. "But so be it." Bhishma, Vidura, Drona and Kripa watched grimly as preparations were made for the game.

Yudhishthira said: "I wager this pearl and this golden necklace."

"And I," said Duryodhana, "wager these jewels. In a little while they may be yours."

The skilful Shakuni threw the dice on the board. "I win."

"The game was hardly an honest one, but never mind," said Yudhishthira. "I wager the whole of my royal treasure against yours."

Again Shakuni won.

"I wager my royal chariot, covered with tiger skins, ornamented with golden bells and banners, and drawn by eight white horses."

Shakuni won.

"Then I wager a thousand young slave-girls with golden bracelets and necklaces, trained in the sixty-four arts and skills."

Shakuni won.

"I wager all my servants, dressed in silk."

Shakuni won.

"I wager a thousand huge elephants the colour of grey clouds, each with six females."

Shakuni won.

"I wager a thousand war chariots with teams of horses and warriors, each of which receives a thousand gold pieces a month."

And again Shakuni won.

"Now I wager ten thousand carts pulled by other beasts, bulls, buffalo and mules, and six thousand broad-chested foot-soldiers."

This time, too, Shakuni won the game.

Vidura leaned uneasily over towards Dhritarashtra: "Listen to me, O king, lord and master, though my words may be as bitter as a medicine offered to the dying. When Duryodhana was born, he brayed like a donkey and howled like a jackal. I told you then that this son would be the doom of your house. Tell Arjuna to kill him. Sacrifice the crow, so as to win the peacock. Sell the dog, to buy a tiger. Drive out Shakuni, who is known for his false play!"

"I know whose side you are on, Vidura," said Duryodhana, who had overheard. "You have never liked us, and we did not know we were nursing a viper at our breasts. You are like a whore! Be off with you! Go!"

But Vidura went on speaking to Dhritarashtra: "Treacherous mouths speak sweetly; but you, King Dhritarashtra, must bite the bitter pill of truth and come to your senses, while there is still time!"

But King Dhritarashtra was silent and took no notice.

Shakuni asked Yudhishthira: "Have you anything left to wager? Anything that is not ours already?"

"I still have plenty," Yudhishthira replied, quite entranced by his passion for the game, and half insane from the

extent of his losses. "I wager all the horses, cows, sheep and goats throughout the territory between the Rivers Yamuna and Sindhu."

And again Shakuni won.

"I wager my capital city, the whole of my kingdom, and the property of all my subjects except for the Brahmans."

Shakuni won.

And Yudhishthira, when he had nothing left at all, went on to lose his younger brothers Nakula and Sahadeva, then Arjuna and Bhima.

"You have lost everything, Yudhishthira," noted Shakuni, drily. "What have you got left?"

"I still have myself," said Yudhishthira, stubbornly. "I wager myself."

Shakuni gave a surly laugh, and threw the dice. He won. "Now you can wager only Draupadi. Wager her, and you may win yourself back!"

"I wager Draupadi," cried Yudhishthira, like one insane.

"Shame! Shame!" cried the assembled kings. Karna, Duhshasana and the other Kurus chuckled gleefully, and Vidura sat dejected, his head in his hands, staring numbly into space. Bhishma, Drona and Kripa had tears in their eyes.

Shakuni deftly threw the dice. Silence fell, with only the sound of the dice rattling across the board. "I win!" cried Shakuni. "I win again!"

"Go, Vidura," said Duryodhana proudly, "and bring Draupadi, beloved

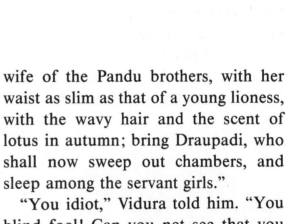

wife of the Pandu brothers, with her waist as slim as that of a young lioness, with the wavy hair and the scent of lotus in autumn; bring Draupadi, who shall now sweep out chambers, and sleep among the servant girls."

"You idiot," Vidura told him. "You blind fool! Can you not see that you are treading the edge of a precipice?"

"Then *you* go, Duhshasana," said Duryodhana, turning to his younger brother. "You bring Draupadi, since Vidura is ashamed. Drag her in, for she is now our property, the same as these here." And he pointed disdainfully to the Pandus with his left hand.

The jubilant Duhshasana burst into Draupadi's chamber. "We have won you, Draupadi! Now you are ours! Put aside your modesty, and come and join us."

Draupadi could not believe her ears.

"First Yudhishthira lost his riches and his kingdom, then his brothers and himself, and now he has lost you," cried Duhshasana, joyously. "Come along, then, now you belong to us!"

Draupadi covered her pale face with her hands and said in a whisper: "Leave me alone, and do not touch me. I cannot go anywhere. It is my time of the month, and I must not go among men."

"No matter what time it is," Duhshasana retorted rudely, grabbed her by her clothing, and dragged her by force into the gaming room, though she begged him and struggled, and shook like a banana tree in a gale.

With hair tousled and clothes untidy, Draupadi stood humiliated and shamed in front of the men assembled in the gaming room. In her heart she called upon Krishna to help her, but out loud she said: "There are among you old and wise men. What say you to this, that I have been dragged here roughly, against my will, and disgraced? Why are you all silent?" And she looked at the Pandus, who stood there in an embarrassed dilemma, not knowing what to do.

Duhshasana was still holding on to her, and he cried out: "Slave-girl! Slave-girl!" And Karna, Shakuni, Duryodhana and the other Kurus laughed in amusement.

Bhishma said: "This is a difficult situation. How could Yudhishthira wager Draupadi, when he had already lost himself? And what is more, Yudhishthira said nothing about Shakuni cheating. As I say, it is a difficult situation."

Then Dhritarashtra's son Vikarna spoke up. "Our teachers Drona and Kripa are silent. Vidura, too, says nothing. What is your opinion? I think that when Yudhishthira had lost himself, he had no right to wager Draupadi, who is the wife of all the Pandus. Draupadi was not lost, either according to the rules of the game, or according to the moral order."

"Not so fast," objected Karna. "No one seems to agree with you. Was

Draupadi not Yudhishthira's property before he lost her? Do you really think it is against the moral order to drag in the wife of five men? The gods allow a woman one husband only. Even if we were to strip her naked, no one might be offended. Have we not won everything which belonged to the Pandus? Does it not all belong to us? And we can do what we like with that which is ours. Well, then, let us strip her!"

Duhshasana grabbed a corner of Draupadi's clothes and began to pull them away. In desperation and shame Draupadi again remembered Krishna, and called out loud: "Krishna, spirit of the universe! Help me!"

Then a thing never seen or heard of before occurred: however much cloth Duhshasana tore from her body, there was still as much on it as before. But Duhshasana went on pulling, and there was soon a great pile of fine cloth on the floor. The kings laughed at Duhshasana's vain efforts, and clapped their hands merrily.

"I swear," cried the mighty Bhima, rising and clenching his fists, "and mark well my words, that in the great struggle that will one day break out, I will tear Duhshasana's breast open with my bare hands, and drink his blood!"

There was silence, and Duhshasana sat down sheepishly beside the pile of crumpled cloth. Draupadi, still dressed, hung her head in shame, and said quietly: "The old and wise in this assembly have not yet answered my question — do they consider what is being done to me to be right?"

And Bhishma said: "I repeat, matters of the moral order are exceedingly complex. It is a difficult affair. Ask Yudhishthira whether he lost you or not."

"Well, then," Duryodhana joined in, "tell us, Yudhishthira: is Draupadi ours, or isn't she?" And, exposing his left thigh, he showed it to the unhappy wife of the five Pandus.

Bhima rolled his eyes threateningly, and roared: "You wretch! In the great struggle which will one day break out,

I will break that thigh of yours in half!"

In the distance the howling of jackals was heard; the donkeys in their stalls began to bray, and birds of prey cawed ominously. Vidura leaned over to Dhritarashtra to draw his attention to these unpropitious signs.

Dhritarashtra said: "My sons have gravely insulted the wife of their relatives. Fate surely has retribution in store for them, for each of our deeds bears fruit, as every cause has its effect. Virtuous Draupadi, speak your wish, and I will fulfil it."

Draupadi lifted her tear-filled eyes and whispered: "Let Yudhishthira be freed so that none may say my son Prativendhyu is the son of a slave."

"So be it," said Dhritarashtra. "Yudhishthira is free. What other wish do you have?"

"Let Bhima and Arjuna and the twins Nakula and Sahadeva be free also, and their arms and chariots returned to them."

"Let it be," said Dhritarashtra. "It is already so. What more do you ask?"

"It would be too much," objected

Draupadi. "Thank you. If the Pandus are free, they will see to the rest themselves."

"How sure you are of yourselves!" commented Karna, but no one took any notice of him.

Yudhishthira went up to Dhritarashtra and bowed to him with his hands clasped before his forehead. "What are your orders, my lord?" he asked.

"Go in peace," said King Dhritarashtra. "I am blind and old. I allowed this game of dice because I wished to try my sons, to test their virtues and vices. These I now know perfectly. I have seen that they are envious, intolerant and proud, and take no notice of good advice. You, Yudhishthira, are honourable, Arjuna is patient, Bhima is valiant and Nakula and Sahadeva respectful and obedient. Return to Indraprastha, and be noble and virtuous, as you have always been."

The Pandus made ready to leave, but Duryodhana, accompanied by Shakuni and Karna, went up to Dhritarashtra and said to him persuasively: "Father, allow us one more game! Just one more throw of the dice!"

And the weak, compliant King Dhritarashtra allowed them one more game, ignoring Vidura's protests.

Yudhishthira said: "It is the will of fate. I know I shall lose, but I cannot refuse the challenge." And he returned to the board.

Shakuni explained to Yudhishthira that they would play for exile. It was a strange wager. If the Pandus lost, they would have to spend twelve years in exile, and a thirteenth somewhere where no one would recognise them; otherwise they would risk a further twelve years' exile.

Yudhishthira pursed his lips, but he accepted the conditions of the game. "Well, then, let us begin," cried Shakuni, the old trickster.

He shook the dice, and with a cunning grin threw them onto the board. "I win again!" he chuckled, maliciously.

The game was over.

Exile in the Forest

When the Pandus and Draupadi left to go into exile in an unknown place,. leaving old Kunti and Draupadi's children behind at the court in Hastinapura, Dhritarashtra called his counsellor and brother Vidura, and asked him:

"What shall we do now, dear Vidura?"

"Why do you ask?" replied Vidura, calmly, "when you take no notice of my advice? I told you when Duryodhana was born to bring about the ruin of your house. Now I advise you that Duryodhana, Shakuni and Karna should go to the Pandus and persuade them to return, and that Duhshasana should apologise sincerely to them and to Draupadi before an assembly of courtiers. That is my advice, though I do not expect you to take it, since it is surely not to your liking."

"You speak only on behalf of the Pandus," objected Dhritarashtra, "but I do not agree with you. Though the Pandus are almost like my sons, Duryodhana and the others are my own flesh and blood. I love you, Vidura; are you not my younger brother? But do not offer me advice like this."

Vidura left the king an embittered man, muttering to himself: "This house is doomed to destruction." And he set out in the footsteps of the Pandus and their wife Draupadi.

Meanwhile, the Pandus had left the banks of the holy Ganges and trekked to Kurukshetra, the fields of the Kurus; they bathed in the cleansing and cool waters of the Yamuna and the Saraswati, then walked on to the deep western forests, where they lived among the birds, the wild beasts and the holy hermits. It was there that Vidura found them.

They greeted each other joyfully, and Vidura said: "My counsel is as

bitter to King Dhritarashtra as a strong medicine given to a sick child."

Then Vidura told the Pandus what was happening in Hastinapura, adding: "I do not like it there. The atmosphere is stale, unpleasant and gloomy. Dhritarashtra's dynasty is coming to an end; I can feel it in the marrow of my bones. And that end will be a cruel one."

"We are to live in these forests for twelve years," Yudhishthira told his brothers bitterly, "and all through my fault. Twelve years of solitude. Let us choose some pleasant spot where there is plenty of game, birds and woodland fruits, and where the holy men and penitents go. Come, let us settle beside the lake in the forest of Dwaitavana." So they went to the forest of Dwaitavana, and made their home there.

One evening Bhima said: "What have we to gain by staying here in exile? Dhritarashtra won our kingdom by cunning and trickery, as a jackal may steal the prey of a mighty lion. Why do we not take arms and win back our realm by courageous battle?"

"You are right," said Yudhishthira. "Your words prick me like arrows, but I will not complain. It is I with my foolishness who am the cause of the exile you must endure. I know this better than anyone. But I must remind you again, that the observance of the moral order and the fulfilment of all its obligations, and the performance of the tasks set by fate are more grave and more important than life itself."

"Life is short, brother," objected Bhima. "It vanishes like the foam on the waves of the sea. In the thirteen years which will pass before we are allowed to return, we shall be exactly thirteen years closer to death. What sort of patience do you call that? We must act at once! Come, we will fight the Kurus, and kill them!"

But Yudhishthira disagreed, and took up a resolute stance against violence. It was not out of vacillation, or from fear or cowardice; he knew that there is a time for all things, and that when the great struggle broke out, it would be too late for long preparations.

He called Arjuna, and with a smile said to him: "Dear brother, in Hastinapura there are several excellent men learned in the arts of warfare, who are skilled in all weapons and in the principles of defence and attack; the chief among them are Bhishma, Drona, Karna and Kripa, though there are others. Take my sword and my bow and arrows, and go towards the north. Nothing must stop you. In the foothills of the Himalayas you'll do penance, and live in privation. The king of the gods, Indra, has in his power all the divine weapons, which were committed to his care by the other gods. Ask him for them, and he will give them to you, for so it was foretold by the wise holy man and holy sage Vyasa."

Arjuna did as Yudhishthira told him; he took his leave of his brothers and their wife Draupadi, and set out for the north. He passed through many lands, overcame many dangers, until finally he reached Indra's palace, and bowed humbly before the king of the gods. Indra greeted him most warmly, and offered him a seat on the edge of his magnificent throne. Arjuna was as radiant as a second Indra, and Indra himself could not take his eyes off him. Son and father glowed with a heavenly brightness, like the moon and the sun of the last day of a dark fortnight and the first day of a light fortnight. The *gandharvas,* or heavenly singers, sang in unison, and played all manner of

instruments, and the *apsarases,* the nymphs, danced enchantingly; incomparable among them for their beauty and elegance of movement were Menaka, Gopali and Urvasi.

Though Arjuna already had all the heavenly weapons, even the fearsome and terrible thunderbolts of Indra, at the invitation of the king of the gods, his own father, he stayed on in Indra's paradise for a full five years, enjoying all the delights and entertainments of the gods.

Indra, king of the gods, soon saw that the beautiful *apsaras* Urvasi had caught Arjuna's eye, and he told the chief of the *gandharvas,* Chitrasena:

"Go to Urvasi, the best of the *apsaras,* and tell her I wish Arjuna, who is already skilled in all arms and knows all the principles of defensive and offensive warfare, should learn the finer points of the art of love."

And Chitrasena did as he was told. He said to Urvasi: "You have surely already noticed Arjuna, that handsome, courteous, disciplined, valiant, clever, modest and honourable young man. Indra wishes him to try all the delights of this paradise. And he surely likes you. Show him your favour!"

Urvasi only smiled, for this order was not, as was said in those days, *pratiloma*, which is as much as to say that it was quite in keeping with her own wishes. She bathed herself thoroughly, rubbed herself with sweet ointments, and sprinkled herself with perfumes. She bedecked herself with jewellery, and round her neck she placed a garland of flowers. Her clothes were as transparent as the clear rays of a full moon. As soon as twilight came, she set out to visit Arjuna.

Arjuna went out to meet her, and greeted her with all the honours which befit beautiful women and nymphs. "I am your slave, Urvasi," he told her, and in this way won her over right from the start.

"Whenever I danced, Arjuna," Urvasi said gently, "you had eyes only for me. I like you too, and I danced as if there were no one watching but you. I fell in love with you, and I have come to you to consummate the joy we both long for."

Arjuna looked confused. "No, no!" he cried. "You are a heavenly nymph, and I cannot compare with you! I honour you like my own mother, like Indra's wife Shachi. I liked the way you danced, and could not take my eyes off you. Indeed, whenever I see you, you fill my eyes and my thoughts. But you are the first mother of the house of Puru, though you do not grow old and are always a young girl. You are related to me, and can have only maternal feelings for me."

"Arjuna, you must understand that I am not a human woman! I am a heavenly nymph, an *apsaras*," Urvasi insisted. "I am free to do what I will. My sons and grandsons the Purus have already enjoyed me. Do not refuse me, do not reject me. I love you. Make me your own!"

"No, Urvasi, please! You are for me like my mother; consider me your son. I fall down on my knees!"

Urvasi considered this refusal a grave insult, for it was the first time she had ever been rejected. She was seized with rage. Her eyebrows puckered; she threw back her head like a wild mare, and cursed Arjuna: "You have disdained a girl who came to you not only on the orders of your father, but also out of love, and for this disgrace you shall spend your life as an impotent eunuch, and no woman will want you again!"

For the ire of a woman scorned is a force to be reckoned with.

Arjuna told Indra of this, and Indra comforted him: "Blessed be the mother of such a modest and virtuous son! Do not worry, Arjuna, I will limit Urvasi's curse to one year, to the thirteenth of your exile. It will be of use to you then, mark my words."

And so it was to be.

When Arjuna did not return for so long, Yudhishthira said to his brothers: "We are quite out of humour without Arjuna. This whole forest of Kamyaka-vana is a desert; what use to us are flowers, fruits, lakes, birds and game, when Arjuna is not here with us?"

"Let us go elsewhere, so that we may find diversions, and make the period of our exile pass more quickly," suggested Sahadeva.

So they walked and walked, visited innumerable holy places of pilgrimage, crossed many mountains and forests, waded through many rivers and streams, saw many cities, towns and villages, until at last they came to the holy River Alakananda, which is the source of the holy Ganges. There they performed the ceremony of cleansing, and they would have moved on, only the gentle Draupadi, unused to such long treks, had lost her strength and fainted.

"A difficult journey lies before us,

across mountain passes and forests," said Yudhishthira. "How is our wife to stand up to it? She is not used to such tribulations."

Nakula and Sahadeva, meanwhile, brought Draupadi round with cold water, massaged her, and rubbed her tired feet.

The mighty Bhima suggested: "I could carry you, or, what would be better still, I will call my son Ghatotkacha and his *rakshasas*, and they will carry all of us."

No sooner had Bhima thought of Ghatotkacha, than the latter appeared with his *rakshasas* and bowed to his father Bhima, and right away they picked up the weary travellers and carried them through the air, over mountain and valley, across the holy mountain of Kailasa, on which heavenly flowers were blossoming and heavenly fruits

ripening. At the foot of this mountain, beside a lovely lake, the Pandus thanked Ghatotkacha and his assistants, and settled down there for a time, in the shade of the holy mountain. It was a pleasant spot, but they were soon bothered by evil and importunate demons, who first of all wanted to carry off Yudhishthira, then Draupadi, for they desired her. But the Pandus overcame and killed them all. Time slipped by, and the fifth year of their exile passed.

Then, one day, a ruddy golden flash came from the heavens, like a searing flame. It was Indra's heavenly chariot, driven by his charioteer Matali, and it brought Arjuna, whom they had missed and for whom they had waited so long.

Arjuna greeted his brothers and the dear and faithful Draupadi, and they welcomed him enthusiastically.

"Your mission was a long one, dear brother, but it was successful," Yudhishthira told him. "Welcome back among us, for we have missed you greatly. And now show us the weapons the divine Indra gave to you."

First of all, Arjuna showed the splendid bow called Gandiva, given to him personally by Indra, then all the other weapons of war he had acquired in the kingdom of Indra. When he showed them the power of these weapons, the whole land quivered with terror; the rivers, streams and brooks stopped flowing, and their waters were dead; rocks burst open and mountains collapsed. The wind ceased to blow, the sun grew dark, and fires went out.

Then the divine sage Narada appeared, and said: "These weapons are not meant for display or showing off! They can be used only in the great struggle, when it breaks out, and even then only when there is no other help." And he vanished.

So Arjuna put the weapons away until the great struggle was destined to begin.

When the Pandus were still living by the lake in the forest of Dwaitavana,

they had been visited by a wandering holy man who accepted their friendly hospitality and then went on to Hastinapura. There he told Dhritarashtra and his sons the Kurus how wretchedly the Pandus were living in exile, dressed in poor clothes made of animal skins, and the soft bark of trees. He also told them of the miserable hovel in which Draupadi had set up her household, and how she cooked what fruits the forest offered, or fish from the nearby lake and streams.

Dhritarashtra was saddened, but Duryodhana, Shakuni and Karna did not hide their malicious pleasure. When the holy man had gone on his way, Shakuni said in private to Duryodhana and Karna: "Now they are in the forest of Dwaitavana. What if we were to visit them there in all their glory? Would it not be a pleasant feeling for us in our luxury to look on our cousins living miserably somewhere in the depths of the forest? Let us dress up in our finest clothes and pay them a visit, so that they may burst with envy!"

"What a good idea," Duryodhana replied, enthusiastically. Then he added, sadly: "The trouble is that our father Dhritarashtra will not allow it, I am sure. We shall have to think of something else."

The very next day Karna came to Duryodhana, beaming all over. "What do you think," he said. "My cattle have wandered off, and are grazing close to the lake of Dwaitavana. We shall have to drive them together and bring them back here!"

Duryodhana chuckled merrily. "The king is sure to let us do that!"

And Shakuni, too, laughed. "He may even order us to do so!" he said.

When King Dhritarashtra heard about it, he ordered Duryodhana: "Of course, you must drive the cattle back as soon as possible. But the Pandus are somewhere in that area. Be careful not to upset them, and if possible avoid them altogether!"

Duryodhana pretended not to hear at all. He took with him Shakuni, Karna, Duhshasana and some of his other brothers, wives and other girls, soldiers, horses, chariots, elephants, poets, musicians, jugglers — in short, it was a grand procession, the purpose of which was to irritate the Pandu brothers.

First of all they gathered together the cattle in a place where there was plenty of water, then divided them up into bulls, cows and heifers; three-year-olds were marked, and heifers kept in a separate corral.

But when they wished to make stronger fortifications, and set off into the forest for wood, they came across a guard of *gandharvas*, who blocked their path.

"Out of the way!" cried the commander of Duryodhana's soldiers. "We come on the orders of King Duryodhana, son of Dhritarashtra!"

The *gandharvas* laughed: "Are you out of your minds? Since when have mortals given orders to the denizens of heaven?"

But the soldiers took no notice, and forced their way into the forest. The *gandharvas* told their chief, Chitrasena, and he and his whole army attacked the Kurus. The slaughter was fearful, and the *gandharvas* with their divine weapons came out the victors. Even the brave Karna fled from his chariot, which the *gandharvas* smashed to smithereens, and to save his skin he rode from the battlefield in Vikarna's chariot. Duryodhana fought bravely, and stood his ground in his chariot, but when his horses and his charioteer were killed, Chitrasena himself leapt upon him and took him prisoner.

The noise and turmoil of the battle, and the desperate cries of Duryodhana's fleeing soldiers aroused the Pandus' curiosity. When they saw what was happening, Bhima said: "I like it! At least someone is on our side."

But Yudhishthira interrupted him: "Now is not the time for malice," he said. "The Kurus are crying out for help, and they do indeed need it. Does it matter that we have quarrelled a little? That happens in every family. Forward, brothers!"

Arjuna called out: "Set Duryodhana and all the prisoners free!"

But the *gandharvas* only laughed. "We obey only Chitrasena's orders! We are heavenly ones, and you have no right to give us orders!" With that they flew into the air, taking Duryodhana with them.

The fighting broke out anew. Arjuna shot dozens of arrows into the air, and amputated heads, legs and arms fell back to the ground.

"Have you had enough, Chitrasena?" called Arjuna. "Let Duryodhana go!"

"He is a villain!" Chitrasena replied. "Has he not done enough harm to you?"

But when Yudhishthira entered the fray, Chitrasena changed his mind, and released the humiliated Duryodhana and all the other prisoners. He sprinkled divine nectar on all the fallen *gandharvas,* reviving them. Then they all flew up and disappeared into the air.

"Take your cattle and your people,"

Yudhishthira told Duryodhana, who was sulking angrily, "and go back to Hastinapura."

Filled with rage and shame, Duryodhana led his procession back the way it had come.

"Thank you for the visit; do come again!" smirked Bhima. Duryodhana only bowed his head and grated his teeth.

The next morning Duryodhana woke up late, and in a terrible mood. He was sitting on his bed, scratching his tangled hair in bewilderment and scowling like a moon in the eclipse, when Karna came in.

"I see you have returned alive and well," the latter said, without a word of greeting.

"You do not know how it all finished, since you ran away before the end," Duryodhana told him, sourly. "But in the end the battle against the *gandharvas* was won by the Pandus, and it is only thanks to them — imagine, thanks to them — that I did not remain a prisoner of Chitrasena. I should rather have fallen in battle than returned with such shame on my shoulders. Leave me alone. Life has ceased to give me pleasure. I will fast until I die."

He threw Karna out, spread some holy grass on the floor, cleansed himself ceremoniously with clear water, sat down on the grass and went into meditation. He tried to break off all ties with this world of material phenomena, and longed for eternal salvation.

But at the same time the demonic *daityas* and *danavas*, which live in the space between heaven and earth, had gathered in fear, for they knew that if Duryodhana were to die they would lose their protection from the gods and from the Pandus. They quickly performed a magic ceremony, and using magic spells created a beautiful girl to bring Duryodhana to them. When she had done so, they said to him: "You must not die, since you are our only hope, just as the Pandus are the only hope of the gods. Go back to earth, stay alive, and victory shall be ours."

The magic girl took him back to his bedroom and put him to sleep. Duryodhana slept a deep sleep, and when he awoke he was convinced it had all been a dream. He had quite forgotten that he had wanted to starve himself to death. Though Karna mentioned it to him in jest, Duryodhana did not believe him, saying: "You are making it up! I will defeat the Pandus in the great struggle, when it comes!"

Karna laughed, and said: "That is what I call resolve. Living and fighting, that is what decides matters. But we must make careful and extensive preparations; nothing must be neglected or forgotten."

Duryodhana decided that he would first of all make the great royal sacrifice of *rajasuya*. For this purpose skilled craftsmen forged him a large ploughshare, made entirely of gold, in order that he might plough the symbolic furrow, and the guests began to arrive in Hastinapura.

An envoy also came to the Pandus to invite them to the great occasion. "Not now," Yudhishthira said, declining on behalf of all his brothers. "Now we should be breaking our vow of exile. Tell Duryodhana that it is good that he is going to hold a *rajasuya,* but that we need not attend."

The *rajasuya* was an ostentatious one; holy men were given rich gifts and entertained lavishly; friendly and allied kings had a merry and amusing time, and Duryodhana in his vanity was more drunk with his own glory than from the wine.

When Duryodhana was walking through the gate into the royal palace, some of the citizens waved to him, called out his name and glorified him, threw roast rice at him and sprinkled him with sandalwood perfume. But others looked on in silence, and there were even those who said under their breath: "It wasn't up to much — nothing to compare with Yudhishthira's *rajasuya.*"

But Duryodhana's friends paid lip service to him, saying: "There has never been a *rajasuya* as splendid as yours! You have held the greatest *rajasuya* ever!"

And, blinded by his own self-respect, Duryodhana believed them.

In the Kingdom of the Matsyas

At last the twelve years were up.

Yudhishthira supposed it was time to decide how and where to spend the decisive final year of their exile, so that no one would recognise them. He said to his brothers and their wife Draupadi: "Twelve years have passed, and we have a mere twelve months before us. Where shall we hide during that time?"

"There are many pleasant places where we could live quite contentedly for that year. The kingdoms of the Panchalas, the Chediskas, the Matsyas, Shurasena, Avanti, Mallowa and others, which are not far from here, would offer us a welcome and a pleasant refuge," Arjuna said.

"In my view the most suitable of them," replied Yudhishthira, "would be the kingdom of the Matsyas, where the old and honourable King Virata rules. But let us consider how to get there, and how to announce ourselves when we arrive."

Arjuna asked: "How do you wish to serve King Virata, Yudhishthira? We must disguise ourselves and remain unrecognised."

And Yudhishthira said: "I have thought of that long ago. I shall do what I know best. When I go before King Virata, I shall say: 'I am Brahman Kanka, learned in the art of playing the game of backgammon, something for which I am famous in the lands which lie beside your kingdom. I will play this game with you, and you will not win it often.' Well, you have heard, brothers, what I intend to do at the king's palace. But what about you, brother Bhima, known as Wolf's Stomach? What service will you perform at the court of King Virata?"

Bhima said: "Ballawa shall be my name. And I will tell the king: 'I am skilled in the culinary arts, a cook, to treat your tongue. I cook so ingeniously that even the gourmet is satisfied. I do not cook the same thing twice, but invent and flavour cleverly and add to ordinary foods such spices and sauces that even the greatest epicures find my dishes special.'"

Arjuna said: "I will dress up as a eunuch. Brhannata will be my name. I must grow a long pigtail in order to look the part. It will be no problem for me to hide my manhood at court. Then I will sing the old lays in the bedrooms of women, teach the ladies-in-waiting courtly manners and speech, dancing, singing and all sorts of other odds and ends."

Nakula said: "I will become the chief groom in the stables of the king. It is pleasant work, I fancy, for I am

fond of horses. To care for noble horses, to rear them and cross them with animals of good pedigree, is more than a joy to me. When the king asks me, I will say my name is Granthika. I look after horses well and know how to cure them, too."

Sahadeva said: "I will be a herdsman, brothers, and my name will be Tantipala. You know I can milk a cow quickly, deftly and cleanly. And I know cattle's nature well, and can even handle bulls, and know which of them is better suited to this cow or that. I can tell by the smell of their urine when they are going to calve. This shall be my work."

Yudhishthira said: "This is all very well, only we have a woman in our midst, wife of us Pandus all, who is dearer than life to us. Our charming

They all agreed. Yudhishthira said: "But what are we to do with our arms? We cannot take them with us, or we should give ourselves away, and another twelve years of exile would await us."

"There on the hill, close to the burial ground, stands a tall, thick acacia tree," the observant Arjuna pointed out. "Let us hide our weapons in its spreading crown."

It was a good idea. Nakula climbed up into the acacia and in the strong branches of the thick crown of the tree he hid all the supple bows, sharp arrows and long swords in their ornamental sheaths, in such a way that they could neither fall, nor would it rain on

wife, petite, gentle, graceful and soft, who has never done housework. What could she do now, Draupadi, dear soul, to help us men in this our predicament?"

And Draupadi said: "Do not worry, Yudhishthira! I will tell King Virata: 'I am a skilled hairdresser, suitable for your wife. I will work hard on the queen's black locks, comb them, clean them, create fine hairstyles for her.' That, my husbands, is something which will serve us in good stead."

So everything was settled. And they set off in the direction of the kingdom of the Matsyas.

When they drew near to the capital city, Draupadi said: "I am tired. Let us spend the night here, and we will enter the city tomorrow."

them. Then they hung on one of the lower branches a dead body they happened to find nearby, so that its fearful appearance and repulsive smell might keep inquisitive eyes away.

The next morning, when they entered the royal city and went to King Virata's palace, Yudhishthira led the way.

King Virata noticed him, and asked his counsellors: "Who is this graceful man who comes here on foot and without servants or escort, though he looks like the king of the gods himself?" But none of his counsellors could tell him.

Yudhishthira went before the king and greeted him courteously.

"Who are you?" asked King Virata.

"I am a Brahman; I have lost all my possessions, and come to you to ask for employment and assistance."

"Welcome," said Virata, "but who are you really?"

"My name is Kanka, and I am a good player of backgammon and other games. I am a good friend of Yudhishthira, but since he and his brothers are in exile, he has troubles enough of his own."

"Very well," said the king. "I like experienced and skilful players. Stay here with me, and I will see to your needs."

"But I have two conditions," Yudhishthira replied. "I do not wish, my lord and king, to have any arguments over games with players of lower castes; and if anyone loses to me, let

him not ask to be given back what I have won."

"Very well," Virata agreed. "If anyone insults you or angers you over a game, I will drive him out of my kingdom. He whom you praise shall be rewarded. I wish you to feel at home here."

After that the beautiful Draupadi arrived. Her thick, soft black hair was plaited into a long pigtail, which she had flung over her right shoulder; but she covered it with a corner of her magnificent sari, so that it might not appear too immodest. Queen Sudeshna saw her from the palace terrace, and at once gave orders for her to be brought to her.

"Who are you?" she asked.

"I am a chamber-maid, and a good hairdresser. My name is Sairindhri, and I am also trained in the arts. I should be glad if you could give me work in return for shelter and food."

"I do not know if I should believe you," the queen answered. "You are very beautiful; you have fine ankles and straight legs. Your breasts are full, your hips rounded. You speak well, your brows are arched, your lips red, your waist slim, your neck pearly, and your face like the moon at the full. I cannot believe one such as you would wander the world seeking service for shelter and food. What man could resist your beauty? They would all go mad if you only smiled; especially my royal husband, old though he may be. If I take you into my service, I shall be like the person who climbed into a tall tree, only to fall to the ground and crush his bones."

"Do not worry, O queen," said Draupadi. "Neither your husband, nor any other shall have me. I am married to five powerful *gandharvas,* and if any strange man touches me, he will die an instant and irrevocable death."

"Then I will take you into my service, and I assure you that no one will expect you to eat scraps, and that you will not have to wash anyone's feet," Queen Sudeshna told her.

Then Bhima approached King Virata, disguised as Bellawa, the cook, and requested to be appointed as chef to the court. His wish was granted by King Virata.

The next to appear at the palace gates was a tall, slim man with a handsome face, hung with earrings and bracelets; his hair, plaited into a long pigtail, hung down behind his back. He bowed to King Virata, and said: "My name is Brhannata, and I am a good singer, dancer and musician. I could teach Princess Uttara the art of dancing. But do not ask me to tell you how I come to be a eunuch, for the memory is still too painful."

"I see that you are a talented artist," the king told him. "Then you will be a dancing teacher, not only for Princess Uttara, but for all the girls at court."

None the less, King Virata tested Arjuna's artistic skills, and asked two of the girls of the court to make sure he was really a eunuch. Thanks to the curse of the nymph Urvasi and the kindness of the king of the gods, Indra, even this somewhat peculiar trial turned out well for him. So Arjuna, under his assumed name of Brhannata, was received into the service of Virata, King of Matsya.

And Virata received the younger Pandu brothers equally generously; Nakula became equerry in the royal stables, and Sahadeva started work in the cattle sheds.

Thus the last year of the Pandus' exile began.

It was not an easy year, that last one, especially for the gentle Draupadi, who

had to serve others, though she was a queen herself. Men are able to clench their teeth and close their minds, but women are fragile vessels. Nevertheless, Draupadi fulfilled her duties without complaint and conscientiously, and she was soon a favourite of Queen Sudeshna.

But it happened that Draupadi's beauty did not escape the prying eyes of the queen's brother, Kichaka, Virata's general and commander of the army. "Who is this splendid girl? Why is she a servant?" he thought. Then, one day, he met Draupadi on a palace staircase, and he addressed her:
"Who are you, charming maiden?
I noticed you long ago.
A face like the moon
  on a winter's night,

Eyes like lotus flowers;
Waist as slim as a young lioness's
Weighed down by the weight
          of your breasts.
I desire you, and I want you,
Were I to lose all for you!"

"It is not possible," Draupadi told him firmly. "For I am married to five mighty *gandharvas,* who would quickly make an end of you, if you were to touch me!"

But Kichaka was not to be put off so easily. "Look at me!" he said. "I am young, handsome, and rich. Do as I ask!"

But Draupadi would not hear of it, and ran away.

General Kichaka gritted his teeth: "I'll get you, yet, you imp!" he muttered. And he went to his sister the queen.

"Sister," he told her, "the girl who has just left your chambers is very much to my liking. I want her. You must help me somehow. I beg you!"

Queen Sudeshna wished to help her brother, and she had an idea. At the next feast day she would send Draupadi to Kichaka's house for the day's special foods and drinks. "And once she is there, brother," she smiled, "it is up to you to persuade her and to convince her that you truly love her."

Kichaka thanked the queen, and could not wait for the feast day to arrive. Then, on the queen's orders, Draupadi went to Kichaka's house with a jug and a basket to get the foods. Kichaka greeted her with glowing vanity: "Today is my lucky day! Sit down beside me, and drink some wine. Come along, then, don't be shy!"

"No, thank you," Draupadi replied. "I came only to fetch the food."

"Another servant girl will see to that," the mealy-mouthed Kichaka told her, for he was interested only in having his shameful way with her. He held out his hand.

"I have never been unfaithful to my husbands," cried Draupadi, "and I never will be!"

Kichaka tried to embrace her, but Draupadi slipped out of his arms and ran out of his house into the royal palace. In her fear and desperation she called upon the sun god Surya to help her. He sent in her defence one of the good demons, a *rakshasa*.

Kichaka caught up with her in the ante-room of the royal council chamber. He grabbed her by the hair, threw her to the ground, and kicked her angrily. At that instant the invisible *rakshasa* sent by Surya struck him such a blow that he was knocked unconscious. All this was witnessed by King Virata and Yudhishthira and Bhima, who were speaking with the king at the time.

Bhima wished to fling himself upon Kichaka and punish him on the spot, but Yudhishthira, afraid they would be exposed, held him back.

"Steady, now, cook!" he warned him. "Go and make ready wood for your fire."

Bhima did as he was told, and went out, though his eyes were burning with anger.

"King and master," Draupadi addressed the king. "Kichaka has insulted me in your royal court, and I request justice!"

"I do not know what has happened, nor whose fault it was," said King Virata. "How, then, can I decide the matter?"

"There is a time for all things," said Yudhishthira, stepping in. "Can you not see that the king and I are preparing to play backgammon? Do not disturb us just now!"

"Those damnable dice again," muttered Draupadi through her teeth, and she went out proudly. "That lecher must die!" she thought. She performed the cleansing ceremony, and in the evening, when all were asleep, went secretly to Bhima.

Bhima was snoring like a lion. Draupadi went up to him and spoke as sweetly as a *gandharva's* lute. "Why are you asleep, Bhima? Look at me, at your shamed wife!"

Bhima awoke, sat up, and said: "Tell me all that happened."

"What am I to tell you? You know everything. You saw what happened to me, and yet you sleep as calmly as could be. Yudhishthira saw it, too, yet he calmly plays that stupid backgammon of his. He is a player, you a cook, and Arjuna, with his hair combed like a woman's, is teaching the princess to dance! I am ashamed of you!" And she started to cry quietly.

Bhima sighed. "I wanted to punish Kichaka at once; I should have ripped him apart like a snake, but Yudhishthira held me back. I understand how

offended you are, my dear wife, but believe me, when this last year has passed, you will be happy again."

But Draupadi continued to weep. "Bhima, you must understand that I cannot stand the humiliation. Queen Sudeshna is jealous of me, and that disgusting Kichaka is determined to have me. You must kill him! Or I will take poison, and die before your eyes!" She curled up in his arms, rested her head on his huge chest, and wept her eyes out.

Bhima gently dried her tears, kissed her, and said: "Do not cry. Kichaka will die tomorrow evening. Arrange to meet him in the dancing hall; but it must remain a close secret."

Then they took leave of each other, and Draupadi hurried to her chamber.

Early the next morning she happened to meet Kichaka in the courtyard. "There you are, you see," the lustful fellow said, without greeting her, "not even the king would stand up for you. And if you do not refuse me, I will give you a hundred slaves and a hundred slave-girls."

"But no one must know of it," whispered Draupadi. "If you promise me that, I will come."

"I promise! No one shall know."

"Then meet me after sunset in the dancing hall," she whispered. Kichaka wanted to embrace her, but Draupadi was quicker than he, and she ran off as if she were shy.

That day seemed to Kichaka inter-
minable. He could not wait for the sun
to drop behind the horizon. All afternoon he bathed himself, rubbed himself with perfumed ointments, combed
his hair and adorned himself like
a bride expecting a visit from a rich
merchant.

In the meantime Draupadi went into
the royal kitchen and whispered to
Bhima, who was just adding spices to
a thick sauce: "This evening after
sunset in the dancing hall. Kill him
there! Thank you."

"He will die, be sure of that," Bhima
told her resolutely. Draupadi gave him
a kiss, and ran off.

As evening fell, Bhima dressed up as

a girl, and when it was dark lay down on a couch in the dancing hall. He did not have long to wait. The door creaked, there was a soft shuffling, and Kichaka's muffled voice said: "Here I am, my beauty; I have come to you!"

Bhima felt his hot breath; he leapt up, grabbed Kichaka by the hair with his left hand, and whispered fiercely: "You are in for something a little different to what you have been expecting!" And with his right fist he struck him a fearful blow in the middle of the chest; he hurled him to the ground and leapt upon his stomach with both knees. Then he kneaded the general into a large, bloody ball. Kichaka died miserably and quickly; he did not even have chance to cry out, let alone offer any resistance.

Bhima called Draupadi. "Here you have him, as you wished," he told her. And he went back to the kitchen to his work.

Draupadi ran to the guards and told them: "My husbands the *gandharvas* have killed Kichaka, who made advances to me." The guards rushed into the dancing hall with blazing torches, and saw there the large ball of bloody flesh and bones.

The news soon spread throughout the royal palace, and through the whole city, and a crowd of onlookers gathered round the cooling corpse of the royal commander-in-chief. They gazed in horror at Kichaka, lying there like a dead turtle which had just been dragged out of a lake.

Among those who came to stare were the relatives of Kichaka. "Come along," some of them began to say, "we will burn Sairindhri along with his body!" The members of the family began to crowd around Draupadi, who did not understand what was happening, though she could see hatred and a thirst for vengeance in their faces.

King Virata, who was afraid of internal divisions in his kingdom, was not pleased with the idea, but he gave permission to Kichaka's relatives to take Draupadi away and carry out their awful plans.

So they seized her and dragged her off to the burial ground. Terrified, Draupadi called out for help, wept and shouted, but the other courtiers did nothing to stop what was happening, since they knew that it was not taking place against Virata's will or without his knowledge.

Draupadi's cries reached Bhima in the kitchen. He dropped his pots and pans, dishes and trays, and leapt out of the window. Tearing up a huge tree by the roots, he stripped it of branches and used the trunk to smash the heads of Kichaka's relatives.

"It is her husband, a *gandharva*!" they cried in terror, and ran off in all directions. But to no avail, and soon a hundred and five bodies lay scattered about the place. No one recognised

Bhima in the turmoil, and he was able to return quickly to the kitchen and stop his food from burning.

The courtiers said to King Virata: "Sairindhri is free, and Kichaka's relatives have been killed. She is indeed beautiful, and will be a temptation to others, for men easily fall victim to lust. You must consider what is to be done for the best in this matter."

Virata was startled, and he asked his wife, Queen Sudeshna, to release the hairdresser and chamber-maid, Sairindhri, from her services.

"I should tell her myself," Virata added, sheepishly, "but I do not wish to offend her, since she is protected by the mighty *gandharvas*." He was weak and a coward, perhaps because of his advanced years.

Queen Sudeshna told Draupadi the will of the king, and said to her: "You must leave our kingdom." But Draupadi said: "Very well, I will do so, but not at once. Give me another thirteen days, my lady, and then my husbands, the *gandharvas,* will take me away, and will remember that you have been kind to me."

Throughout that thirteenth year Duryodhana's scouts had combed the length and breadth of the land in search of the Pandus. Do not forget that they had to remain unrecognised, or they would have to stay in exile for a further twelve years. That was the condition. And since Duryodhana did not wish them to return to Indraprastha, he was doing his best to find them. But without success.

"We have found nothing at all, sire," the scouts reported. "There is no sign of the Pandus anywhere. Only at the court of the King of the Matsyas some *gandharvas* killed Kichaka and a hundred and five of his relatives."

"Time rushes by," said Duryodhana to his companions, anxiously. "What are we going to do?"

"Who knows what has become of them?" threw in Karna, carelessly, and gave a disdainful wave of his left hand. "Maybe they have been devoured by wild animals, or have sailed across the ocean. Forget them."

King Susharman of Trigarta, who had been defeated several times at the hands of Virata's army under Kichaka, suggested: "If the *gandharvas* have killed Kichaka, the Matsya army is without a general, and Virata is defenceless. Let us attack his kingdom, which is rich in cattle, and seize his herds."

This idea met with general approval. The Kurus marched into the territory of Virata's kingdom on the seventh day of the dark fortnight; first they planned to drive off rich herds of cattle, then to conquer the rest of the kingdom. The day on which they attacked was the last day of the Pandu brothers' thirteen-year exile.

Virata's army, though lacking a general, marched against the invader. It was late afternoon when battle was joined.

Virata's charioteer was killed right at the start, and the king himself was taken prisoner by Susharman of Trigarta. Yudhishthira tried to persuade Bhima to go to the king's aid. Bhima grabbed a tall tree, in order to tear it up by the roots and use it as a weapon, but Yudhishthira restrained him.

"No, brother, they would recognise us! Fight like the rest, with bow and arrow, sword and battle-axe." And Bhima did so.

Susharman, who began to be afraid, turned to retreat. Bhima called out to him: "Are you running away, then, Susharman, cattle thief and bully of old men?" Susharman could not ignore a challenge such as this, and he returned to the fray.

Bhima leapt down from his chariot,

grabbed Susharman by the hair, threw him to the ground and sat astride his chest.

"Beg for mercy!" he cried.

"Let him go, brother," Yudhishthira told Bhima, "for he is not worthy of your attention. The main thing is that King Virata is free."

Then Susharman left the battlefield in disgrace, and Virata was extremely grateful to his cook and his dice player, though he had no idea who they were.

Nevertheless, Duryodhana and his troops managed to steal and drive away nearly seven thousand cows, heifers and bulls. The herdswomen and herdsmen, when they announced their losses to King Virata, lamented loudly, and poured abuse on the marauders.

Virata's bold son, Uttara, who had fought valiantly in the front ranks, said: "I need only a good charioteer, and I should set out at once in pursuit of the cattle thieves." But all the good charioteers had been killed or gravely wounded.

Draupadi said to Uttara: "Brhannata, the dancing teacher, is also a good charioteer."

But Prince Uttara only laughed. "Am I to make a eunuch my charioteer?" he asked.

"Why not, when he is truly a good one?" retorted Draupadi.

"If you recommend him to me," said Uttara, "then I will take him on; but I will not ask him myself."

"Then let your sister ask him," suggested Draupadi. And so it was.

The slim princess with her firm breasts and rounded hips came to Brhannata, whom we know better as Arjuna, smiled at him, and said: "Sairindhri spoke very well of your skill as a charioteer before my brother. Our situation is desperate. Please help us and drive Uttara's chariot against the marauders."

"Very well, Princess, I will gladly do it," replied Brhannata the eunuch.

The girls of the court giggled till they almost collapsed, then said: "Brhannata, bring us back from the battle pretty dolls and gay ribbons!"

Arjuna took no notice, but went to prepare the chariot and harness the horses. When Uttara sat in the chariot, Arjuna said only two words to him: "Trust me."

Arjuna whipped the horses into a gallop. When Duryodhana's army came in sight, and Uttara saw the armed hosts of surly soldiers turn towards him with their weapons lowered, his courage deserted him.

"I can't do it," he gasped. "I am afraid. Let them all laugh at me, I don't mind. Let them steal the cattle, let them plunder our capital city, if they want to!" And he threw aside his bow and arrows.

"You are of the caste of Kshatriyas," Arjuna reminded him. "Do not forget that death is preferable to cowardice."

But Uttara wanted to flee.

"No!" cried Arjuna sternly. "I told you to trust me! Come with me!"

He drove to the tall, spreading acacia and told him: "Climb into the tree. High up in the crown you will find the mighty weapons of the Pandus. Bring them down, for we are going to need them."

"But there is a body hanging there! I will soil myself!"

"Forget the body; we need the weapons!"

So Uttara climbed the tree and brought down all the weapons which the Pandus had hidden there a year before when they first arrived in the capital city of the Matsyas.

"Whose is this magnificent bow, ornamented with gold?" the prince asked the eunuch. "And whose this heavy sword, bearing the sign of a frog?"

"The bow belongs to Arjuna, and the sword is Bhima's; all these weapons belong to the Pandu brothers."

"Well, but why are we taking their weapons?" asked Uttara. "And where are the Pandus now?"

Arjuna laughed merrily. "Now I can

tell you. I am Arjuna. The court back-gammon player is Yudhishthira, Bhima is the cook, and Nakula and Sahadeva are looking after your horses and cows. And our wife Draupadi is she whom everyone considers to be Sairindhri, the queen's hairdresser."

Prince Uttara gaped in wonder.

"Do not tarry, my friend, but load all the weapons into the chariot," Arjuna told him. "There is a battle before us."

In the meantime, Duryodhana had ordered the stolen cattle to be driven onwards, and was drawing up his battle lines. "I have a feeling," he said, "that Arjuna is near. And since the thirteenth year is not yet up, the Pandus are threatened with another twelve years' exile." And he gave a gloating chuckle.

But Bhishma said: "You are wrong, Duryodhana. The wheels of time turn inexorably, by the hour, the day, the week, the fortnight, the month, the season and the year. No one can slow them down, nor speed them up. The Pandus' period of exile has just expired!"

This made Duryodhana furious, but there was nothing he could do about it.

Arjuna grasped the reins and drove the horses straight at the Kuru army. Over his head fluttered his standard, bearing his symbol, a monkey. Taking the reins in his teeth, he fired off four arrows.

"It is Arjuna!" cried Drona, who used to be his teacher. "See; two of his arrows lie at my feet, and two whistled past my ears. He is greeting me, as it is fitting to greet one's teacher!"

Karna sent a hail of arrows in Arjuna's direction, but he dodged them nimbly, and put Karna to flight with arrows of his own. The rest of the Kuru army also did their best to hit Arjuna, but no one succeeded; only Duryodhana's arrow scratched his forehead a little.

The boastful Vikarna charged at Arjuna on a huge elephant, but Arjuna killed the beast with a single arrow in the temple, and it fell like a rocky cliff brought down by a flash of lightning.

Vikarna ran away like a coward. When Duryodhana saw this, he turned his chariot and began to ride away from the battlefield. But Arjuna pursued him, calling out: "Stop, Duryodhana! Stop, and show us how you can fight!"

Duryodhana, his pride offended, nimbly turned, like a snake when trodden on. He hurled himself at Arjuna, followed by Bhishma, Drona and Duhshasana. But Arjuna rode between them as easily as a crane flies through a cloud, and all the corners of the earth shook with the sound of his war shell, which Arjuna blew merrily. All froze with horror at that sound, and their weapons fell from their hands.

"Hurry up, before they have time to recover themselves," Arjuna told Prince Uttara. "Take the white robes of Drona and Kripa, the blue of Ashwatthaman and the yellow of Karna. But beware of Bhishma, for he is awake."

Uttara did as he was bidden, and Arjuna said: "Our soldiers have already driven back the cattle and shut them in their pens. We can return." And he turned their chariot towards the royal city.

In a while he said to Uttara: "For the time being you are the only one who knows who the Pandus are. Keep our secret, and say nothing to your royal father. Tell him only that you drove back the raiders, and saved the cattle."

The defeated Kuru army beat a humiliating retreat to Hastinapura. "Why did you not shoot at Arjuna?" Duryodhana asked Bhishma, ferociously.

The latter smiled. "I did not think you would collapse at the mere sound of his shell . . ."

When fast messengers told King Virata the news that his herds had been saved, he ordered the musicians to play and the dancers to dance, and sent Princess Uttara out to meet Prince Uttara, so that she might welcome him before he entered the city gates. Then he turned to Draupadi and said: "Bring my dice. I want to play. We shall see what my court player, Kanka, can do."

But Kanka, or rather Yudhishthira, told him: "Games are a delicate business, O king. Have you never heard that Yudhishthira of the Pandus lost everything in a game of dice?"

The king only waved his hand, and made the first throw. As if by the way, he said: "My son Uttara has driven off the Kurus, and taken back the herds they stole from us."

"No wonder," noted Yudhishthira, "since Brhannata was his charioteer."

"What do you mean by that?" demanded the king, angrily. "Are you suggesting, you insolent fellow, that my son needs the help of some eunuch to defeat his enemies?" And he jumped

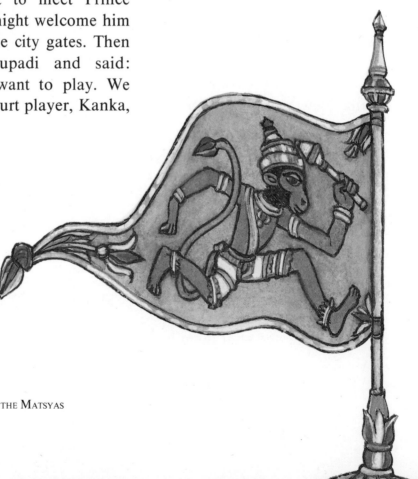

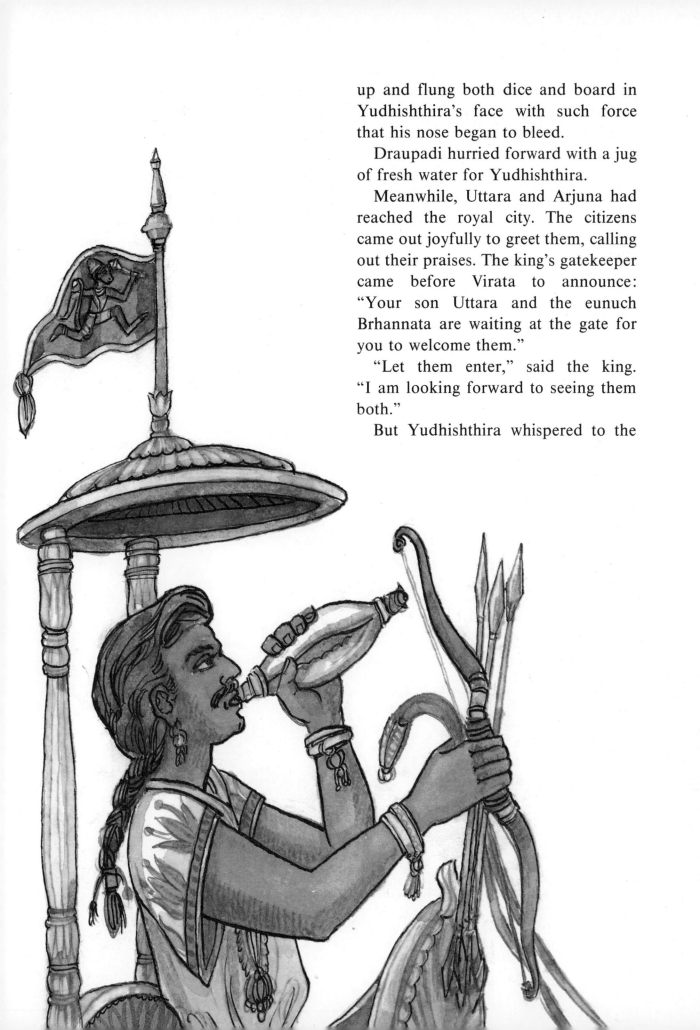

up and flung both dice and board in Yudhishthira's face with such force that his nose began to bleed.

Draupadi hurried forward with a jug of fresh water for Yudhishthira.

Meanwhile, Uttara and Arjuna had reached the royal city. The citizens came out joyfully to greet them, calling out their praises. The king's gatekeeper came before Virata to announce: "Your son Uttara and the eunuch Brhannata are waiting at the gate for you to welcome them."

"Let them enter," said the king. "I am looking forward to seeing them both."

But Yudhishthira whispered to the

gatekeeper: "Do not let Brhannata in! He would kill the king if he saw me bleeding like this!"

When Uttara entered and saw Yudhishthira's face covered in blood, he asked: "What has happened? Who struck him?"

"It was I," admitted the king, "for he wished to give credit for your deeds to the eunuch."

"Alas, father," cried Uttara. "You have done ill! You must beg his forgiveness!"

The king stood up, but Yudhishthira said: "My lord and master, all is forgiven; I forgave you at once, for you do not know all the circumstances."

King Virata was surprised, for he did not indeed know all the circumstances.

He said to his son: "I am happy, Uttara, that you have shown yourself a valiant man, and that you have driven out the conceited Kurus, and saved our herds, without being wounded in battle. This is a pleasantly cool breeze on my old liver."

"It was not I, father," said Uttara. "I wanted to flee the battlefield, but the son of one of the gods stood by me and drove off the marauders. It was he who saved our cattle. And when it was all over, he disappeared. But he is sure to return, perhaps tomorrow, perhaps the day after. Who knows?"

And the day came when the Pandu brothers, dressed all in white, strode into the royal palace like lions entering a mountain lair, and went into the throne room, where they sat on the magnificently carved chairs reserved for guests of royal rank. King Virata still had no idea who they were, and he cried out indignantly: "Hey, Kanka, player of dice, how dare you sit in that chair?"

Arjuna smiled. "He might sit on the throne of Indra himself, O king, for he is not the player Kanka, but Pandu's son Yudhishthira."

Only now did King Virata understand, and he was embarrassed and ashamed. "Pandu brothers, forgive me if I have harmed you in any way, or somehow insulted you. It was done in ignorance." And he looked at his son Uttara, and said: "I wish to conclude an alliance with you, and I will give Arjuna my daughter in marriage."

But Arjuna said: "Sire, I will accept her as my daughter-in-law. She will make an excellent wife for my son, Abhimanyu."

King Virata asked: "Why do you not want her as your wife?"

And Arjuna replied: "Do not consider me ungrateful, O king, but I have

spent a whole year in the women's chambers as the eunuch Brhannata, and your daughter behaved as respectfully to me as to her own uncle. It would not be fitting for me to marry her. It would be easy for unpleasant gossip to spread, and I should like to avoid that."

"You are right," said King Virata. "Then she shall be the wife of your son Abhimanyu."

The wedding was a grand one, and kings and nobles from far and wide attended it. Flutes, oboes, horns, cymbals and drums sounded from morning till night; poets recited verses of celebration, jugglers and tight-rope walkers showed their daring skills, and the dancers did not stop for a moment. King Virata gave Abhimanyu seven thousand swift-footed horses, two hundred elephants, and a pile of gold. He himself made the libation of ghee into the sacred flame, and honoured the Pandu brothers as befitted their station.

The Struggle Begins

When, after several days, the wedding feast was over, the Pandus and all the kings who had been guests at the marriage met in a great gathering in the magnificent council chamber of Virata's royal palace.

Krishna rose to his feet and said: "You all know the conditions which were agreed between Yudhishthira and Duryodhana. When Yudhishthira lost his entire kingdom in that accursed game of backgammon, the Pandus left for thirteen years' exile, and though they could have seized their kingdom by force whenever they wished, they did not do so. That is of great importance. The Pandus have kept their word. But we do not know what Duryodhana thinks of the matter, or what he plans to do now. I therefore propose that we send to him a reliable, noble and honourable man to ask Duryodhana to return to Yudhishthira his seat of Indra-prastha, together with all the Pandus' lands within their original bounds."

"This is a right and just proposal," Krishna's elder brother, Balarama, added. "For we surely do not wish to let loose an armed conflict. We want

peace. Prudence often succeeds where force is to no avail."

"What is the use of words?" asked Krishna's charioteer, Satyaki. "Why should Yudhishthira plead for what is his by right?"

"Because we prefer the ways of courtesy, my friend," Krishna reproved him. "If the Kurus are willing to act honourably, then so much the better. If not, we are prepared to adopt a different course."

The sacrificial priest of King Drupada, a venerable old man who knew how to treat with both men and gods, was sent as an envoy to the Kurus. The gathering of kings broke up, and Arjuna rode away with Krishna and Balarama to Dwaraka, Krishna's seat of government.

But the Kurus' spies brought Duryodhana news of all that had occurred at the royal court of King Virata, and Duryodhana set out at once with a small company to Dwaraka, to visit Krishna; for he had plans of his own.

Krishna was asleep when they arrived, and Duryodhana sat beside the head of his bed. Then Arjuna came in, and stood respectfully at the foot of the bed.

When Krishna awoke, he saw Arjuna first, but Duryodhana blurted out: "I was here first, Krishna, and I ask you for help. You cannot refuse me!"

"I know that you came first," Krishna told him, calmly, "but Arjuna was

the first one I saw. I will help both of you; but the younger has preference. Choose, then, Arjuna, whether you want the whole of my well-armed and well-trained army, without me, or me alone, without my army and without weapons."

Without hesitation, Arjuna chose Krishna himself. The foolish Duryodhana was filled with joy, and at once asked Krishna for his army. Krishna agreed.

When Duryodhana had left in high spirits, Krishna asked Arjuna: "Why did you choose me, when you know I will not fight?"

"I do not need soldiers, Krishna. I want you to be close to me; then I shall be stronger."

"Then I will be your charioteer, and drive your war chariot," said Krishna. "You can rely on me."

When Drupada's sacrificial priest arrived at the Kurus' court in Hastinapura as envoy of the Pandus, he was received by Dhritarashtra, Bhishma and Vidura.

"O king," he addressed Dhritarashtra, "I will not speak of the rights of succession of the Kurus and the Pandus, nor of whether or not the kingdom should be justly divided between your sons and them. But I must emphasise with all gravity, that according to our ancient moral order every agreement must be kept, so long as the conditions laid down by it have been observed, and that what is to be returned must be returned."

Old and good-natured Bhishma said: "We are glad that the Pandus are alive, and that they have survived their time of exile without misfortune. And we are still more pleased that our cousins wish to live in peace."

"Empty words!" interrupted Karna, who was also present. "We know how things stand. And if the Pandus think Duryodhana will give them back everything that Yudhishthira lost just like that, then they are very much mistaken!"

"You speak foolishly, Karna," Bhishma told him gravely. "You do not know what you are saying. Have you

forgotten that Arjuna alone defeated us, when we tried to drive away the cattle of King Virata? Think a little."

Then old King Dhritarashtra spoke: "I must give the whole matter my consideration. You, sacrificial priest, may go. I will send a missive of my own with my reply to the Pandus."

The sacrificial priest took his leave and departed. He was uneasy at heart, for it seemed to him that he might have completed his mission successfully, but that the matter was out of his hands.

King Dhritarashtra called his charioteer Sanyjaya and said to him: "Go to the Pandus and speak sweet words to them. Promise nothing, and above all try to find out what their plans are. But take care not to upset them. You should be especially cordial towards Krishna, for the Pandus never do anything without his blessing."

Sanyjaya bowed, and set out for Dwaraka to visit the Pandus. "I bring a message from King Dhritarashtra," he told Yudhishthira and the other brothers. "He praises your honour, your modesty and your wisdom. He says that you always know what is right and just, and what is not. He knows that you are aware that to commit evil is to soil the honour of the family, and he begs you to act only in the interests of your house."

"That is all very well," replied Yudhishthira, "but King Dhritarashtra speaks as if we were guilty of something. You know the whole truth about our relations with the Kurus. We always hope to live in peace and friend-

ship, but we remain the same Pandus we have always been. We demand that Dhritarashtra return Indraprastha and our kingdom, and we demand it by right, since the conditions have been fulfilled."

"Why are you so eager?" asked Sanyjaya. "Wrath is a poor counsellor. Is it not better to be patient?"

"Indeed it is," Yudhishthira agreed. "Patience is better: but our patience has endured a long time; I trust you have not forgotten how to count the years. But where men mix up their ideas of right and wrong, and where injustice is passed off as justice, there is no place for patience. Ask Krishna here what he thinks, for he has seen both sides of the coin. I will abide by his advice, for he is a noble and just man."

And Krishna said: "Sanyjaya, you surely know that I want the Kurus and the Pandus to live in peace and prosperity. We are all related, after all; we all belong to the same house. But I cannot close my eyes to some things which are very obvious. Can you deny that the Pandus have suffered thirteen years of exile? Can you deny that Duryodhana wants the whole kingdom for himself? Do not suppose, Sanyjaya, that you know better than Yudhishthira or I who is in the right. Do you suppose the Pandus have forgotten how Duhshasana dragged Draupadi into the gaming room and wished to strip her naked? Or that they have forgotten all the deep insults they have suffered undeservedly at the hands of the Kurus? Tell Dhritarashtra that we wish to preserve peace, but not at any price!"

"Then live in peace and contentment," said Sanyjaya. "I will tell the king."

"And above all tell him this," said Yudhishthira firmly, "that he should return to us Indraprastha and all our territory, or he should make ready for war!"

Kurukshetra, which means the field of the Kurus, is a broad plain which stretches between the Rivers Saraswati and Drishadwati. There the Pandus and their army pitched camp in a spot

which offered plenty of water, fodder and firewood. Krishna had a long and deep ditch dug and filled with water, and behind it he placed the tents for the soldiers, provisions and spare weapons. At the rear of the camp there soon appeared traders' stalls with all the things soldiers may need, and the tents of physicians and surgeons, together with craftsmen of various trades, above all smiths, armourers, saddlers and shoemakers. The Pandus' camp grew larger day by day, as the troops of allied kings and mercenaries poured in. On one side of the camp the horses were stabled and the chariots assembled, while on the other side the war elephants stood. Special tents held supplies of weapons, spears, lances, arrows, clubs, slings and axes, vessels of boiling oil, venomous snakes, fire arrows and torches.

The very next morning the Kuru army set up camp opposite. Each chariot had four stallions harnessed to it, and on each elephant sat seven warriors. For each chariot there were ten elephants, for each elephant ten horses, and for each horse one rider and ten foot soldiers.

"An army without a commander is a senseless and unruly crowd," Duryodhana told Bhishma. "Take command of us."

And Bhishma replied: "You know that I love the Pandus as well as I love you. But I have given my word, and I will command your army as I have promised. Now we must agree who is to lead the first attack — Karna or I, for he is sure his skills as a soldier are quite the equal of mine."

"As long as Bhishma is able to fight," said Karna, "I will abide by his orders."

So the general of the whole Kuru army was to be Bhishma, great uncle of the warring cousins, of both the Kurus and the Pandus.

The evening before the great struggle began, it suddenly began to rain blood, and the ground turned red; comets flew back and forth unpropitiously, and the jackals howled fearfully. The omens were all bad.

The next morning, after cleansing themselves and offering sacrifices to the gods, the two armies raised their standards and marched off to begin the great battle. The sound of thousands of war shells rent the air, thousands of drums and tympani beat, and the soldiers yelled like wild beasts to stir up their courage for the fratricidal struggle which was now unavoidable.

The two belligerent armies rolled towards each other like two stormy seas at the end of time. Fighting and warfare had strict rules, which no warrior who valued his honour would dare to

break. Soldiers were allowed to attack only adversaries whose equipment was the equal of their own, and to fight honourably and without trickery under all circumstances. He who surrendered out of fear or prudence, or who ran away out of cowardice, was to be spared. No warrior was to take advantage of his enemy's unreadiness, or of the fact that he had dropped or lost his weapon. No one might attack those who begged for mercy or who were retreating, nor charioteers, provisioners, cooks, physicians and nurses, drummers or trumpeters.

When the two glowering armies drew close, the wise holy man Vyasa said to the blind Dhritarashtra: "The time of the great battle is at hand, my king and son. If you wish to see it, blind though you may be, I will give you the power of miraculous vision. Do you wish it, Dhritarashtra?"

"Who would wish to see his relatives, sons, nephews and others murdered in a merciless battle? Not I. Yet I should like to know how the battle progresses, and what is happening on the battlefield."

"Very well," said Vyasa. "I will give the power of miraculous vision to your charioteer, Sanyjaya, who will tell you everything. The slaughter will be fearful; all the signs of fate which I have observed were unfavourable. The hawks and eagles croaked, the crows cawed malevolently, and the her-

ons and cranes sat uneasily in the very crowns of the trees. The moon and the stars shone at the same time as the sun, and on the night of the October full moon the moon did not come out at all. The statues of the gods in the temples perspired and bled. Cows gave birth to donkeys, and the young of all kinds of animals were born with two heads, four eyes, five legs or two tails. The end of the world is near."

King Dhritarashtra sighed heavily: "Thus it has been spoken; thus shall it be."

The great struggle was at hand. Duryodhana told his brother Duhshasana: "Tell the warriors in the chariots to protect Bhishma as they advance. He has vowed not to kill any woman, and Shikhandin in a previous life was born as the woman Amba. I should not like a jackal such as he to slay the lion Bhishma. Do not let him out of your sight! Yudhamanyu will watch Arjuna from the left, Uttamaudjas from the right. As I see, Arjuna wishes to cover Shikhandin. Take care, therefore, that he does not come close to Bhishma!"

Yudhishthira told Arjuna: "There are more of them than there are of us. I propose we form a wedge. What do you think?"

"Indeed. And Bhima shall be at its point," Arjuna replied. "He will break up the enemy ranks as a tiger scatters a herd of gazelle."

"But shall we defeat them, when they are led by the wise Bhishma?" asked Yudhishthira, uncertainly.

"Krishna is with us," replied Arjuna. "We will be victorious."

The soldiers' weapons rattled, the straps of harnesses creaked, and the bells on the war elephants tinkled and jangled. Captains and their lieutenants gave crisp orders, and horses champed at their bits and scraped at the ground, which was damp with the early dew. Flags and banners fluttered in the morning breeze like the flames of the sacrificial fire as the priest pours on the ghee. And the ranks of the Pandu warriors, whose commander-in-chief was Draupadi's brother Dhrishtadyumna, hurtled towards the Kuru army like a herd of mighty elephants, the only escape from which is to run nimbly to one side.

The charioteer Sanyjaya, endowed with wondrous vision, told all this to the blind King Dhritarashtra, whose soul was weighed down by a great sadness.

The great struggle began just before noon. The twanging of bowstrings was drowned by the din of war cries; the wheels of chariots trundled along, and the bells on the elephants rang merrily to the creatures' wild trumpeting. The clash of sword against sword, and against the hard skulls of adversaries, which cracked like coconuts, echoed across the whole of the Kurukshetra. As the great struggle progressed, Bhishma broke through the Pandu defences, helped on both wings by the kings allied to the Kurus. His banner flapped victoriously in the hot midday breeze. Arjuna's son Abhimanyu rode out in his chariot against the Kurus' allies, trying to weaken Bhishma's forces in the flank. But Bhishma did not waver from his attack, and shone out among his troops like a clear-burning, smokeless flame.

When the first day of the great struggle ended with the setting of the sun, the tired Pandu forces retreated,

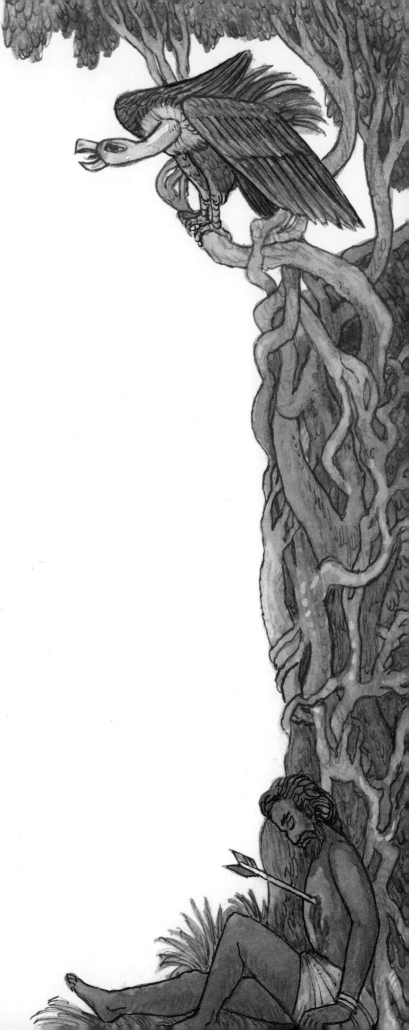

leaving a victorious Bhishma in command of the field.

Yudhishthira entered Krishna's tent accompanied by his brothers and other leaders in the army, and said urgently to Krishna: "Bhishma is destroying us as fire sweeps through dry grass. Help us, Krishna!"

"Stay calm and remain patient," Krishna reassured him. "The commander of your forces is Dhrishtadyumna. And according to the prophecy, Dhrishtadyumna is to kill Drona. Shikhandin is also on our side — and he is to kill Bhishma."

This made Yudhishthira somewhat less anxious. As the council continued, Dhrishtadyumna suggested that the next day they should adopt the formation of a flight of curlews, with Arjuna at its head.

When the battle broke out anew the next morning, Bhishma was again at the head of the Kuru forces. Arjuna's chariot headed straight for him, for Arjuna had told Krishna: "Drive me right to him! I will meet him in combat straight away, and kill him, before he kills us all!"

"That is right, Arjuna," Krishna told him. "But be very careful."

Bhishma fired nine arrows at Arjuna, and Arjuna replied with ten. But that was only the beginning: thousands of arrows flew back and forth, and none of them struck its target, for they all met in mid air. And the two of them continued their duel, testing each other's skill and dexterity, each being truly gratified to see how well the other fought.

At sunset Bhishma turned to Drona with a smile: "Friend," he said, "Krishna and Arjuna are a difficult nut for us to crack, and the men are surely tired. Give the order to retreat."

The fighting was over for that day, and all the soldiers longed to bathe, to refresh themselves and to sleep.

On the third day the Pandus deployed their troops in Garuda's formation, which means that the centre formed a massive block the shape of an eagle's beak, with mighty wings on either side. Bhishma led a fierce counter-attack against their ranks. It was a fearful encounter. The Kurukshetra shook with the thunder of war elephants, the roar of the fighting armies, the clash of arms, the rumble of drums, and the piercing shriek of war shells.

"Stop!"

"Have at you!"

"Here I am!"

"Watch out!"

"I am ready!"

"Strike him!"

"On the left, on the left!"

Severed heads rolled across the battlefield, bloody limbless bodies lay everywhere, their arms and legs scattered around them. War chariots

hurtled past, elephants thundered by.

The wide field of the Kurus
Is steeped in the blood
Of warriors, slain in the heat
Of that dreadful battle.
The vultures gather round them,
Round those valiant men,
Whose blood gushes into
The troughs of the other world.

No one had seen or heard of a battle so cruel. Those who were mortally wounded cried out their last words, then collapsed, and their bodies grew cold and stiff.

Bhishma, heedless of the tumult of battle around him, fired one arrow after another into the Pandu ranks. His chariot drove across the battlefield from side to side, seeming to be everywhere at once, as if there were many chariots, all with Bhishma standing in them, firing his arrows again and again, sometimes two or three at a time. And every one of them found a victim. The Pandu forces were terrified. Their warriors were falling like moths circling a dancing fire.

Krishna said to Arjuna: "Be careful! The Pandu soldiers are confused, and they are losing their will to fight! Now is the time to act, and I suppose you are the one to do it! You must attack Bhishma in this confusion, and put an end to his excesses!"

"Drive towards Bhishma," cried Arjuna. "I will strike him at once!"

And Krishna, who was shining like the midday sun, whipped the horses towards Bhishma. The latter showered Arjuna's chariot with a hail of arrows, but Krishna skilfully drove through it, though the horses were slightly injured. Arjuna drew back *Gandiva,* his mighty bow, and with a single arrow knocked Bhishma's bow from his hand. Bhishma deftly grabbed another, but Arjuna knocked that, too, from his hand with a well-aimed shot.

"Bravo, Arjuna!" cried Bhishma. "Well done! It's a pleasure to fight against you. Fight on, Arjuna, and fight hard!"

Krishna drove the horses in complicated circles, to avoid Bhishma's arrows and to spoil his aim, but some of the arrows hit both Krishna and Arjuna, so that with their bleeding wounds they looked like roaring bulls in a fierce tussle, wounded by their rivals' sharp horns.

Krishna could no longer restrain himself. He stopped the team of powerful stallions, jumped down from the chariot, and shouted: "Arjuna, I am going to attack Bhishma with my disc!" In his right hand the bright disc gleamed, its edge sharper than the blades of all the barbers in the world together. As he ran in huge leaps towards Bhishma, the ground trembled and rumbled ominously.

"Come on, then!" called Bhishma to him. "Come on, god of gods, with your

disc! Slay me in my chariot! What could be more glorious, Krishna, than death at your hands? I will be renowned and glorious in all three worlds!"

"You are the cause of today's carnage!" shouted Krishna. "But you will live to see with your own eyes the death of Duryodhana, and the victory of the moral order."

"Fate is fate," said Bhishma, softly.

But Arjuna, too, had leapt down from their chariot; he ran to Krishna and grabbed him from behind with both arms, so that Krishna could not move. He tried to escape the embrace, but in vain; Arjuna dragged him back as a gale carries off an uprooted tree.

When Krishna ceased to struggle,

Arjuna let him go, bowed to him, and said: "Control your anger, Krishna. I swear I will do all that I have promised, and that I will fulfil the role fate has given me."

Krishna calmed down, jumped into the chariot, grasped the reins, and blew loudly on his war shell.

On the fourth day of the battle the mighty Bhima and his company at-tacked the war elephants of the Kurus and killed their guards and drivers. The elephants, maddened and frightened by the attack, ran off in all directions like dark storm clouds driven by the wind.

Enraged at this, Duryodhana ordered a counter-attack, and the Kurus flung themselves at Bhima and his men. Kuru arrows flew towards them like the waves of an angry sea on

the night of a full moon, and the dust thrown up by the feet of charging soldiers was like a sandstorm in the north-western desert. But Bhima stood his ground, and fought off the foot-soldiers' attack with his club; those who were in chariots he first dragged out, then killed. Dead enemies lay all around him, like the trees of a forest felled by a storm around some massive rock.

With a cunning grin, Duryodhana fired three arrows at Bhima, which knocked the club from his hand. A fourth struck Bhima in the chest. He fell to his knees in pain, then fainted. But Abhimanyu and other Pandu heroes hurried to his rescue and rained arrows upon Duryodhana. At the same time Bhima's son Ghatotkacha and his men flung themselves against the Kurus, and the latter had to retreat.

The battle was continued with the same ferocity and with unfailing resolution, day after day. On the fifth day Bhishma drew up the Kuru army in the formation of a crocodile with open jaws, but even this tactic failed to bring the desired effect. On the sixth day the fighting was mainly between the chariots and the horse cavalry, and again Bhishma was outstanding among the ranks of the Kurus. In the evening the Pandus held a long council to discuss what tactics they might adopt to decide the issue.

On the morning of the seventh day there were only minor skirmishes, but after midday it was Yudhishthira, the eldest of the Pandu brothers, who was lord of the battlefield. He hit the Kuru ranks as a cruel storm strikes fields of ripening crops. It was a terrible sight. Streams of blood flowed across the battlefield. Screeching demons and evil spirits feasted on the bloodied bodies, breaking open their skulls and eating their brains, still warm. Those who managed to save their lives washed their wounds in healing extracts, or waited outside the tents of the physicians to have their injuries treated. Others gathered round the stalls with wine and various refreshments, while yet others visited the dancers and wandering whores. Poets and singers recited songs of glory and ancient ballads, musicians played on all manner of instruments, and priests offered sacrifices and libations to the eternal gods. No one spoke of war, of fighting or of the battle. When, late that night, animals and men lay down to sleep, silence and a transient peace reigned at last on the field of the Kurus.

On the eighth day of the great battle there was a cruel encounter between the fierce Duryodhana and Bhima's son Ghatotkacha. The fight did not last long, though, and soon Duryodhana was forced to retire, much the worse for wear. In fact, he had to give up.

He resented the humiliation bitterly, and called a council, at which, among other leaders, were Shakuni, Duhshasana and Karna, and they tried to dream up a strategy which might lead to the Pandus' defeat. But they came up with nothing new.

Frightened horses ran back and forth across the battlefield with chariots that had lost both charioteers and warriors. Soldiers of all ranks, noblemen and ordinary soldiers, who had fallen that day with mortal wounds, lay there lifeless, their souls having been tied up by the god of death and destruction, Yama, who carried them off to the underground world of the dead. Everywhere were the remains of broken chariots with shafts, axles and wheels smashed; there were the severed limbs of fallen soldiers, once-beautiful heads with manly rings in their ears, weapons of all kinds, some of them broken, others

still usable, leather finger-guards, torn banners, cut-through harnesses and reins, dead elephants and horses.

And Bhishma attacked once more. Encouraged by his fighting spirit, all the Kuru soldiers threw themselves forward anew. No one took account of father, brother or friend. Relationships, friendships, honour and favour all went by the board, and all who could still hold a weapon beat at the enemy in a frenzy, heedless of whom they killed, provided they killed someone, and were not killed themselves.

The Kurus reached the top of a rise, and the Pandu forces began to thin out, their soldiers losing courage and the will to fight on, and running off in all directions.

"Now you must strike," Krishna told

Arjuna, "or it will be too late, and all will be lost."

"I am ready to do as you advise me," Arjuna replied. "Drive my chariot against Bhishma."

When the Pandus saw Arjuna's chariot driving into the attack, they took heart and rejoined battle. One of Arjuna's arrows with a blunt point broke Bhishma's bow in half, and when Bhishma reached for another, Arjuna broke it in half with another arrow before Bhishma even had time to string it.

"What a good shot you are, Arjuna!" Bhishma cried. "I like to fight against you!" And he set against him a shower of arrows with crescent-shaped points, which were capable of cutting through the hardest of skulls. This took Arjuna by surprise, and he hesitated for a moment. Krishna was afraid how the encounter might end, so he leapt from the chariot to attack Bhishma himself, roaring like a maddened lion, his yellow clothes billowing behind him like the lightning during the season of rainstorms.

"Come, Krishna," Bhishma cried, gleefully. "Come and do me the honour of grappling with me! I look forward to it!"

But Arjuna again held Krishna back by force, dragging him away from Bhishma. "Do not be angry with me," he said. "But you said you would not fight. I will kill him myself!"

Without a word, Krishna turned back, climbed into Arjuna's chariot, and took hold of the reins. In the meantime twilight had fallen; the battle around them had subsided, and the armies had returned to their camps.

At the Pandus' council that evening, Yudhishthira said bitterly: "Old Bhishma has hold of our soldiers like an elephant king holding a bunch of dry twigs. Is there any use in fighting on? It is hopeless. I have had enough."

"Go to Bhishma," Krishna advised him, "and ask him how he can be killed. If you ask him personally, he cannot fail to advise you, for he is a guru."

That was a good idea. Krishna and his five brothers, the Pandus, put aside their arms and quietly and without weapons visited Bhishma in his tent in the Kurus' camp.

"Welcome, all of you," Bhishma addressed them, evidently pleased they had come. "You, Krishna, and all you Pandus, Yudhishthira, Arjuna, Bhima

and the twins Nakula and Sahadeva. What brings you here? What do you want of me?"

Yudhishthira told him outright: "Tell us, Bhishma, how we can win this great battle. How can this senseless carnage be ended? Tell me how I may overcome and kill you!"

And Bhishma replied: "You cannot be victorious while I am alive. As long as I can hold a weapon in my hands, not even the gods can defeat me, let alone mortals. The moment I lay down my arms, even a two-year-old puppy could lay me low. And I do not fight against women, against unarmed soldiers, or against cowards. There is one in your army called Shikhandin, who was in a previous life born a woman — she was Amba, daughter of King Kashiske. You surely know all this. If you place Shikhandin in the forefront of your attack, I will not defend myself against him, for I will not take up arms against a woman, even if she was so in a previous life."

The Pandus had heard all they needed to hear. After they had paid Bhishma the honour and respect he deserved, they took their leave of him and departed.

But Arjuna said to Krishna: "I am ashamed, Krishna, for he is my guru also. When I was a child I used to sit on his knee, and he played with me. I called him father, and he always corrected me, saying he was not my father, but my great uncle — the brother of my grandfather. How can I now make ready to kill him? I cannot do it! Never!"

But Krishna told him: "And what of your vow? Have you forgotten that every man must perform the deeds which fate has set before him? Where is your discipline? As it is written by fate, so it must be. And what is written is *kartawyam kuru:* do your duty!"

"Very well," said Arjuna. "But place Shikhandin in front of me, that *he* may be the cause of Bhishma's death."

The next day, too, brought slaughter on both sides. The ranks of the Pandus thinned out, whereas there seemed to be as many Kurus as ever. Even the sun was loath to look upon that dreadful slaughter; it turned away its face, and seemed to be hurrying to the west more quickly than was usual at that time of year.

On the tenth day of the great battle old Bhishma felt a peculiar sensation of disgust. He said to himself: "I am tired. I have had enough of this killing. Soon I will give up, for I do not even want to live any longer."

Arjuna attacked him, standing in his chariot, behind which Shikhandin was hidden. Carefully, he looked out, and sent ten arrows against Bhishma. He struck him in the chest, but Bhishma only looked at him with eyes full of

wise sadness, and did not lift his weapon.

"Now!" Arjuna encouraged him. "You are the only one who can defeat Bhishma. Now is your chance!"

Shikhandin hesitated. But Bhishma took no notice of him, firing his arrows at Arjuna. Duryodhana told several of his men to harrass Arjuna from several sides at once, so that Bhishma would have a better chance of hitting Arjuna.

Arjuna not only defended himself deftly, but attacked swiftly. Angrily, Bhishma grabbed a spear and threw it at him. It flew towards Arjuna as straight as a thunderbolt, but Arjuna awaited his chance, then, setting five arrows in his bow at once, fired them at

Bhishma's spear, which they splintered.

"There is no point in going on — this is a senseless struggle," thought Bhishma. "Arjuna has the support of Krishna, and I cannot take up arms against Shikhandin. The time has come for me to make use of the gift my father gave to me when he married Satyavati — that I might decide the hour of my own death."

And just as he was thinking these thoughts, Shikhandin struck him in the chest with nine arrows, which were quickly followed by twenty-five shot by Arjuna. Bhishma stood proud and motionless, like a mighty rock in an earthquake. Then the arrows were without number; they entered his body everywhere, striking all one hundred and seven mortal spots.

Bhishma swayed slightly. He turned to Duhshasana, smiled a little, and said: "The arrows which went through my breastplate were shot by Arjuna, not Shikhandin. Only Arjuna knows how to shoot through tough armour, like the winter wind which can penetrate even a cow's hide."

"Attack him!" shouted Yudhishthira, and they all flung themselves at Bhishma, the rallying-point of the Kuru forces. Bhishma fell from his chariot, his face turned towards the east, just before the sun set in the west. As he fell, the earth shook. His body was shot through from all sides with so many arrows that it did not even touch the ground, but lay there on a bed of arrows.

And a heavenly voice was heard on high: "He is dead! Bhishma, greatest of the warriors, is dead!"

"I am not dead yet," cried Bhishma. "I am still alive! I will die when I wish to."

The goddess Ganga, Bhishma's

mother, sent holy men to her son in the shape of a flock of golden geese, which flew from Lake Manasa and surrounded his strange bed of arrows. They twittered to each other: "Why must he die at the time of the winter solstice?" And they flew away to the south.

"I shall not die at the time of the winter solstice, golden geese," said Bhishma, raising his head in the direction in which the geese had flown off. "I may choose the time of my death, and I will live on until the spring equinox!"

The two armies laid aside their weapons, and sad warriors with grave faces gathered round the wounded Bhishma. Pandus and Kurus paid him honour and respect, as was befitting.

"Noble warriors, god-like heroes,

I greet you," Bhishma told them. "But my head is sinking. I need a pillow."

They gave him a pillow of down with a silk cover. Bhishma simply smiled. "I need a pillow for a fallen hero, not one so soft I cannot even feel it," he said.

He turned to Arjuna. "My head is

sinking, Arjuna. Give me a hero's pillow," he told him.

And Arjuna said: "Your wish is my command." Setting three arrows in his mighty bow, *Gandiva,* he drew back the string and pierced Bhishma's skull with them.

"Thank you, Arjuna," whispered Bhishma, with satisfaction. "That is what I needed. That is how all warriors of the Kshatriya caste who fall in battle should take their rest. On this bed of arrows I will lie until the coming of the spring equinox. Then I will take leave of this life, as one might take leave of a good friend."

Surgeons, versed in the use of ointments and medicaments, and skilled in removing arrows from the body, gathered round. But Bhishma told Duryodhana: "Make them gifts of gold, and send them away. I do not need doctors. I have achieved the greatest happiness a Kshatriyan warrior can hope for. When you lay my body on the funeral pyre, put it there with all the arrows I am resting on now."

The evening drew on, and all were still standing around Bhishma. He sighed: "Arjuna, I am thirsty. Give me water."

But there was no water anywhere. Arjuna placed an arrow in his bow, *Gandiva,* and with the words of a sacred spell on his lips fired it as far towards the south as he could. The moment the arrow fell to the ground, sinking into the damp earth, a spring of clear water gushed from Bhishma's bed of arrows, and he drank his fill.

"Do you see?" he said to Duryodhana. "Who else could do that but Arjuna? Tame your foolish wrath and suppress your clumsy hatred; stop this senseless fighting! Put an end to this terrible murder of relatives and friends! Give back to Yudhishthira and his brothers Indraprastha and the territories which belong to them, that peace may reign in our land when I am dead!"

But Duryodhana scowled darkly, and all the Kurus and their soldiers made their way back to their camp.

"Now leave me alone," Bhishma asked the Pandus. "I want to enjoy the calm of the night. You know I always tried to keep the peace, and that I was not able to because the Kurus, above all Duryodhana, were too stubborn, envious and niggardly. I take my leave of you, and wish you a good and quiet night before the next day of the battle."

Taking their leave of him, the Pandus and their warriors left, deep in thought.

The Battle Ends

"Bhishma, our wise old man and experienced general, is dying," Duryodhana told Karna, gloomily. "An army without a commander is like a ship without a helmsman, like a chariot without a charioteer. An army without a commander is good for nothing; it suffers one defeat after another, until it is finally brought to its knees, defeated and dispersed. Who should be our commander now? What do you think?"

"Any one of us might take over the leadership of the army right away," Karna replied. "We are all courageous, clever, of good family and skilled in warfare. But I think Drona should become commander, since he is our teacher. We all honour him, and no one will object if he takes Bhishma's place."

Duryodhana agreed. When the Kurus held their council of war, he addressed Drona thus: "Drona, Bhishma is dying, and we have no commander. Take over the leadership: lead our troops into the great battle, take us to victory like a son of the god of war. We will follow you as wild buffalo follow the leader of the herd!"

And all the Kuru soldiers began to proclaim the glory of Drona and of all the Kuru brothers.

"I know well the teaching of the four *Vedas* and the six branches of science," Drona replied. "I know the mysteries of human decisions and deeds, and I know how and when various weapons should be used. If you are willing to put your trust in me, I will gladly lead you in this great struggle against the Pandus."

And on the morning of the eleventh day he hurled himself at the Pandu ranks like the god of death and destruction himself. "You have honoured me with command of the army," he called to Duryodhana, "so tell me what your wishes are, and I will fulfil them!"

Duryodhana took counsel with Karna and Duhshasana, and then shouted to Drona: "Capture Yudhishthira, and bring him here alive!"

"Why do you not wish him dead? Do you have feelings of affection for him?"

"No, but I want him alive!"

"Very well, I will take him alive, but you must distract Arjuna's attention somehow, so that he does not go to his brother's aid. Arjuna was my best pupil, and learned much of the art of warfare from me. Not only that, but he has divine weapons from the god Indra himself!"

And Drona drove into battle with a fury as if a huge river were gushing onto the battlefield: its mighty rush was his wrath, its waves his soldiers; its waters were the hot blood and tears of pain shed by fallen warriors, its whirlpools the war chariots with their frantic teams; its banks were the horsemen and the elephants, its water-lilies the breastplates and shirts of mail, its mud the bloody severed limbs, its froth the fallen helms, and its fishes the spears and arrows that went whistling by; dead bodies tossed about in it like uprooted trees, chopped-off heads rolled along like rocks, hair trailing like water weeds. The loosened wheels of chariots bobbed about like turtles, war-clubs were like crocodiles, and the hosts of

little arrows like shoals of tiny fish. In that mighty flood thousands of warriors were carried to the home of Yama, god of death.

But Drona did not reach Yudhishthira.

And when night fell, the two armies ceased fighting and withdrew to their own camps.

Duryodhana gave orders for the Kuru army to adopt a circular formation, and in the front ranks he placed ten thousand kings with golden banners, sworn to fight till victory or death. All had scarlet garments, scarlet jewels and ornaments, and wore golden necklaces. At their head stood Dhritarashtra's grandson, Lakshmana, who led them straight against Arjuna.

In the middle of the circle stood Duryodhana, shaded by a white parasol, and around him stood Karna, Duhshasana and Kripa; a little way off stood Drona's son Ashwatthaman, and the thirty-three sons of Dhritarashtra.

Yudhishthira put Arjuna's son Abhimanyu in charge of the counter-attack. "Cover Arjuna, and support him," he told the young man. "It will not be easy to break their formation; perhaps we will not be able to. I am relying above all on you, on Arjuna, on Krishna and on Pradyumna. But no one is as skilled in battle as you are. We must break up the Kuru circle, come what may!"

"My father taught me how to break a circular formation," said Abhimanyu. "But I may not return from it."

"Go, and come back also," Yudhishthira told him. "We are right behind you."

Abhimanyu's charioteer whipped up the team of three-year-old stallions, and the chariot, with Abhimanyu standing firm upon it, rushed towards the Kuru circle. Karna's younger half-brother ran forward, and fired ten arrows at Abhimanyu; Abhimanyu set in his bow a single arrow with a blunt point, and with it severed his adversary's head. Karna retreated, and Abhimanyu charged towards the other kings.

Karna's retreat threw the Kuru ranks into confusion. Some soldiers were advancing, while others were in retreat, and they even fought among themselves. Into the mêlée rode the bold Abhimanyu in his chariot, destroying his enemies as a steppe fire consumes clumps of parched grass. Only the Sindhu king Jayadratha and his company stood their ground against the advancing Pandus, but to little avail.

Karna pushed his way through the warring throng to Drona, and said: "Abhimanyu is causing havoc! His arrows are like the lightning when the first storm breaks in the season of rains. Our soldiers are retreating: they are fleeing!"

"Abhimanyu is young and courageous," Drona said. "His weapons are excellent, and his armour cannot be pierced. I taught his father Arjuna, and I see that the son is no less skilled in fighting than his father. Though we cannot defeat him in open combat, we could cut the reins of his team, or kill his charioteer, or knock the bow from his hands."

This advice was of great use, and Karna took good note of it. He himself knocked Abhimanyu's bow from his hands with a single arrow, Kritavarman killed his horses, and Kripa shot his charioteer. Abhimanyu leapt down from his chariot, now useless, and, armed only with sword and shield, rushed at his enemies. It was as though the king of the birds, Garuda himself, were swooping on them. But Drona's arrow snapped Abhimanyu's sword in half, while a cloud of arrows from Karna's bow smashed his shield to smithereens.

Abhimanyu quickly bent down, grabbed the club of a fallen warrior, and set about Drona's son Ashwatthaman, who was standing nearby. But Ashwatthaman became frightened, jumped down from his chariot, and took to his heels. Duhshasana's son went for Abhimanyu, and their clubs crashed against each other as if two ferocious demons were fighting each

other with the pine trees of the Himalayas, which they had pulled up by their roots.

For a long time the combat was evenly matched. But then, as Abhimanyu tried to knock Duhshasana's son's feet from under him, the latter brought his club down on his adversary's head with such force that Abhimanyu, already exhausted by his efforts, fell and died, like the head elephant of a herd, hunted down and killed by a crowd of hunters.

He lay on the field of battle
Like the sun behind the hills,
Like mists lying in the valleys,
Like the moon at the eclipse.

Deeply grieved by their loss, the Pandus withdrew to their camp. In that sad evening twilight, to the dreadful howling of jackals, the sun set. It made night in that place and day in another, taking with it the gleam of swords, shields, arrows and all the weapons and ornaments of war, the metal parts of the chariots and the horses' harnesses, and the tinkling bells with which the elephants were hung.

Soon after sunset Arjuna and Krishna returned to the Pandu camp, where they found their comrades sitting in grief-stricken silence around the flames of a camp-fire.

"Why are you so silent and pale?" Arjuna inquired. "What has happened? And where is Abhimanyu? I cannot see my young and obedient son, with his big eyes and his broad smile. I want to tell him that I was victorious, and have killed Bhagadatta."

"He has fallen in battle, brother," Yudhishthira told him sadly. "He has fallen, and died."

Arjuna sat down, dejected. "What will his mother, Subhadra, say? Why did it have to be him?"

But Krishna comforted him. "Death is the lot of all warriors who do not flee the battlefield. Do not grieve, for his soul has achieved happiness."

"How could you have left him without protection?" Arjuna chided. "Where were you all? I should not have left him alone! If only I had known!"

He stood up and clenched his fists.

"I will kill them all — as long as my strength holds out! I will kill them, and their horses, their elephants, their relatives! I swear by your death, my son! And first of all I will kill Jayadratha."

He picked up his might bow, *Gandiva,* and twanged its string. The sound filled the heavens and its echo rang out over the whole land. Krishna blew his war shell, and Arjuna blew his, making the flesh of the Kurus creep as they listened in their camp.

Early the next morning the Kuru camp was boiling with fighting spirit. Soldiers tested their bows, refilled their quivers with arrows, tightened their bowstrings, put new edges on their blunted swords and war-axes, and weighed their clubs in their hands.

They were making ready for another encounter with the Pandus, and they cried out with great bravado:

"Where is that fellow Arjuna? We'll show him!"

"Where is that famous strongman Bhima? Let him see that we are stronger!"

"Where is Krishna, with his divine might?"

Drona said to Jayadratha: "Take Karna, Ashwatthaman, Shalya, Vrshasena and Kripa with you, a hundred thousand horsemen, sixty thousand chariots with warriors and charioteers, fourteen thousand elephants, and place them some miles behind my troops.

When the time is right, you will attack."

Jayadratha was satisfied; he assented, and did as Drona had commanded.

The wrathful Arjuna attacked the Kurus with ferocity, and broke through the infantrymen in their front ranks. His arrows brought Kuru soldiers down in their hundreds, and the enemy faltered.

Bhima noticed that Karna was crouching down and hiding behind his charioteer. He leapt down from his chariot and grabbed hold of Karna's banner. Karna could not tolerate this humiliation, jumped out from his hiding-place, shouting like thunder

from a storm-cloud, and made ready to attack Bhima. Bhima grabbed everything that was to hand, the wheels of broken chariots, the thigh bones of dead horses, and hurled himself at Karna. But there was no duel between them, for Bhima remembered that Arjuna had promised to kill Karna and thus he retreated; they could not kill each other, even though they dearly wished to. They merely exchanged a few selected insults, rude and to the point, to be interrupted by the arrival of Arjuna in his chariot, who put Karna to flight with a couple of arrows.

"Now, dear Krishna," said Arjuna, "drive me straight to Jayadratha. There is not much time left before the sun sets."

Arjuna's war chariot inspired terror in the Kuru soldiers. With two arrows placed in his bow at once, Arjuna toppled Jayadratha's banner and his charioteer's head.

Krishna, though he was driving Arjuna's chariot, had watched attentively all that was happening on the battlefield. He said to Arjuna: "Jayadratha is covered by six bold kings. You will have to kill them first to get to him. But I will help you. I will use my magic powers to make Jayadratha think the sun is setting, and he will stop fighting, suspecting nothing. Then it will be easy for you to kill him."

"Yes, I will kill him," said Arjuna. Suddenly, twilight fell. All the Kuru soldiers saw the last rays of the setting sun, Jayadratha among them.

Krishna glanced at Arjuna. "Now is your chance," he said. "He is looking to the west. Cut off his head with an arrow, but be careful it does not fall on the ground, or your own head will be smashed to pieces in an instant!"

Nervously, Arjuna wet his lips; he stretched his bow, and with a single arrow cut off Jayadratha's head, as when a hawk snatches a sparrow from the top of a tree. The curse of King Vriddhakshatra, the father of Jayadratha, prophesied that whoever caused the head of Jayadratha to fall to the ground in battle would suffer the fate of a fragmented skull. Aware of this, Arjuna fired off more arrows, which lifted the head high above the Kuru army, until it fell into the lap of Vriddhakshatra. At that moment, as Vriddhakshatra rose from prayer, his son's head fell to the ground, and his own head burst open with a loud noise and shattered to a thousand pieces.

Drona's will to fight and his skill in the use of all types of weapon were causing the Pandus great tribulation.

"He cannot be defeated in battle," said Krishna to Arjuna, "unless he himself lays down his arms. We must use subterfuge. Drona will stop fighting as soon as he hears his son Ashwatthaman has been killed. That is how we will defeat him."

Arjuna did not like the idea, regarding it as dishonourable, but all the other Pandu leaders agreed to the plan, although Yudhishthira did so only with hesitation and after lengthy consideration.

Bhima sought out among the elephants one which also happened to be called Ashwatthaman, and killed it with his thunderous club. Then he ran towards the Kuru camp, shouting:

"Ashwatthaman is dead! Ashwatthaman is dead!"

Ashwatthaman was indeed dead, but it was the elephant and not Drona's son. Drona, however, was not to know that.

In desperation the father, robbed (as he thought) of his only son, flung himself into battle with a vengeance. He fought relentlessly: his weapons struck down twenty thousand Pangchali warriors in their chariots, five thousand Matsya infantrymen, six thousand soldiers on elephants, and ten thousand horsemen.

But then the holy men and priests Vishwamitra, Jamdagni, ·Bhardwaja and many others appeared on the battlefield and told him: "You should be ashamed of yourself, Drona! You, a Brahman, and you are fighting here like a Kshatriya. Remember the holy teaching of the *Vedas,* and tread the path of the moral order, or your pilgrimage through life will be at an end."

The unhappy Drona, prostrate with grief, turned to Yudhishthira, who he knew would never tell a lie even to gain dominion over all three worlds, and asked him: "Is Ashwatthaman really dead?" Eagerly and desperately, he waited for a reply.

Krishna quickly whispered to Yudhishthira: "If Drona remains alive another half a day, he will disperse the Pandu troops to all corners of the

earth. A lie which saves lives is not a lie. To lie to women, or to save priests, holy men or cows is not a sin."

"He will believe you," added Bhima, quietly.

So Yudhishthira, anxious to win the great battle, lied to his teacher, crying: "Ashwatthaman is dead!" But he added quietly: "He was an elephant," so that he should not lie so brazenly.

Drona, hearing of the death of his son from the lips of a man whom he believed, lost interest in everything in this world, even the great battle. Nothing made sense to him any longer. He cast aside his weapons and, committed into the hands of fate, stared into the distance.

Bhima looked meaningfully at Dhrishtadyumna, and said to him quietly: "Now! Now is the moment! Kill him, quickly!"

Drona whispered: "If my son is dead, then I, too, wish to die. I will not touch arms again!" And he sat down on his chariot, bowed his head, and was lost in meditation. He just whispered now and again: "Ashwatthaman, Ashwatthaman . . ." His spirit had already left this world, but the only ones who knew it were Sanyjaya, Arjuna, Krishna and Yudhishthira, who were close by, and Ashwatthaman, who was far away, though still very much alive.

Then Dhrishtadyumna rushed forward and cut off Drona's head with a single blow of his sword. Arjuna

yelled: "No! Do not kill him! He is our guru!" But it was too late. Dhrishta-dyumna picked up the severed head by the hair, and flung it at the feet of the Kurus, who ran off in all directions. Only Ashwatthaman pushed his way through to where his father's body lay, like a ferocious crocodile swimming against the stream.

Drona's death smote the Kurus hard. It cut deep, even into their hard hearts, as if they suddenly felt the whole burden of fate. Duryodhana quickly summoned a council of all the kings, commanders and chiefs, and, trying to encourage them, spoke to them thus:

"I began this great battle because I have faith in your strength and fight-ing skills. But now you look as if you had lost all hope and self-confidence. Why is that? All warriors know that it is either victory or death which awaits them. There is no third way. So fight! Karna is with you, and his mighty weapons, too! So, fight on! Let the Pandus flee before us as a herd of shy does flees from a roaring tiger, taking their fawns with them!"

His words were the right ones at the right time. And Duryodhana went on: "Our two generals, Bhishma and Drona, have fallen. We must decide what we shall do next. Give your opinions; tell us what you suggest."

"Desire, occasion, resolve, skill and thoroughness are the prerequisites of success," said Ashwatthaman. "But even they are subject to fate. Many of our soldiers have fallen, many are gravely wounded. Yet we need not give way to dark despair. If Karna becomes our commander, victory will be ours, for he is a mighty warrior and an invincible hero."

A murmur of agreement ran through the council, and Duryodhana turned to Karna. "You have heard for yourself, Karna," he said, "and I would add that Ashwatthaman has expressed my own thoughts. I know your abilities, and I value your friendship. I should like to make full use of both of them in this great battle. Take over command of our army, Karna, for I am convinced that you are even stronger than Bhishma and Drona were."

"I once promised you that I should defeat the Pandus and Krishna," Karna replied. "I gladly accept the leadership of the Kuru forces. The Pandus may consider themselves dead." His words were very boastful, but they had the required effect on the gathering.

When the battle ended that evening, Karna came to Duryodhana and said: "Tomorrow I will fight with Arjuna, and one of us must fall; either he, or I."

"Do as you see fit," Duryodhana re-plied. "Our horsemen and archers will cover and support you." Then he sent for King Shalya and told him: "Noble King of Madra, serve as Karna's charioteer tomorrow, I beg of you."

Shalya glowered and said indignantly: "You insult me, Duryodhana! Why should I, who am certainly better in all things than Karna, serve as his charioteer?" And he made as if to leave.

But Duryodhana held him back. "Wait a moment," he said. "Do not be angry." He spoke soothingly. "You are right that you are better. But we need your help. Karna is better than Arjuna, and you are better than Krishna. No one can handle a team of horses like you."

"Very well," Shalya agreed. "I am rewarded by your words. I will drive Karna's team. But on one condition: that I may say to Karna's face whatever I want."

"You may, Shalya," Duryodhana assented. "And thank you for accepting."

"Wish me much good fortune, for I will drive the team as best I can. And Karna must not be angry if I say anything unpleasant. Whatever I might say, it will be meant in the best way, and it will be from the heart."

"I will not be offended," smiled Karna.

In the morning, as soon as the sun rose, Karna said to Shalya: "Now drive me to where the five Pandu brothers are. I will crush them like lice!"

"You misjudge the Pandus," Shalya objected. "Do not forget that they are bold, experienced and skilful warriors. You may change your ideas when you hear the twang of Arjuna's bow, *Gandiva*."

"Get a move on!" grunted Karna. "Into battle!"

When they reached the battlefield, Karna went on boasting: "When I get started, once I get going, not even the god of death can save Arjuna, even if he wanted to. Not even all the gods can save him."

"You are a braggart, Karna, and you are proud," Shalya told him, jerking the reins. "And pride comes before a fall. You hold your head a little too high, and you speak out loud that which you should not even think. And

what is worst of all is that you believe it yourself."

"I have heard a great deal about Arjuna and Krishna," Karna replied, somewhat offended. "I have heard much about the Pandus, and know many things about them; but I have yet to hear anything which really impresses me. I will put up with your foolish words, since I have promised not to be offended. But now get on with it! Forward!"

Arjuna stood on his chariot, drawn by stallions as white as doves, and surveyed the Pandu troops, who were forming up under the command of Draupadi's brother Dhrishtadyumna. The Panchala troop attacked the Kurus like a flock of swans descending on a woodland pool; but in an instant Karna cut off the heads of seventy-seven soldiers. Ten heroes in their chariots surrounded him and set upon him fiercely, but they all fell.

Shalya drove Karna's chariot up to Yudhishthira, and Karna slew all who stood in its path. Then, with a mighty blow, he smashed Yudhishthira's chariot to pieces. Yudhishthira quickly jumped into another chariot and began to drive away. But Karna drove up alongside him and shouted disdainfully: "Are you fleeing, Kshatriyan warrior? Then run! Run to Arjuna and Krishna! I do not kill small fry like you!"

Then he cried to his charioteer Shalya: "Now take me to Bhima!"

Bhima saw Karna drawing near, and he told Satyaki and Dhrishtadyumna: "Follow Yudhishthira and cover him. He has just escaped almost certain death."

"Bhima is angry," Shalya said to Karna. "See how fiercely he is standing there, ready to curse you with the most terrible curse he has been harbouring in his bowels for many a year."

An arrow from Karna's bow broke Bhima's in half. Deftly, Bhima grabbed another, placed a heavy arrow in it, and drew the string back to his ear. The terrible blow knocked Karna uncon-

scious, and Shalya quickly turned the chariot and drove his team away.

Duryodhana sent his brothers to cover Karna's retreat, and to attack Bhima. They hurled themselves upon him like bees on a bear stealing their honey. Bhima had already slain fifty warriors in their chariots, and he stood as firm as a rock. The noise of battle was like the roar of many stormy oceans, yet above the din the twang of Arjuna's bow, *Gandiva,* could be heard.

Meanwhile, Karna had come to his senses and was riding into battle again, clutching his huge bow with its gold bands.

That afternoon Karna charged the Pandu forces with ever-increasing fury. Arjuna told Krishna: "Take me closer; we shall see . . ."

Shalya noticed Arjuna's approach, and he warned Karna: "Look, here comes Arjuna with his white stallions. He seems to be coming our way. Now show what you are made of, for you are no worse a man than Bhishma or Drona."

"Well, at last I like the way you speak," said Karna with satisfaction. "Such words are pleasing to my ear."

In the meantime, a little way off, Duhshasana hurled himself at Bhima. His very first arrow, bound with gold and decorated with diamonds, hit Bhima so hard he fell unconscious into his chariot. But in an instant he came round, grabbed his club, and shouted in a fearful voice: "You take an arrow to me, but I will take a club to you!" And, swinging the club mightily around his head, he threw it with all his strength at Duhshasana. The blow flung Duhshasana ten bow's lengths from his chariot, where he lay on the ground, writhing with pain.

Bhima reminded himself of how the malevolent Duhshasana had once dragged Draupadi into the court in Hastinapura by the hair, when Yudhishthira lost her at backgammon, and how Duhshasana had wanted to strip off her clothes before the gathering of

kings and noblemen. The memory of
this intense insult stirred up his fury
still more, as a fire flares up when ghee
is poured into it. Drawing his sword,
he leapt upon Duhshasana. Placing
a foot on his neck, he sliced open his
chest and took a sip of his blood. Then
he chopped off his head and drank
again. Looking around him, he proclaimed with gratification: "Sweeter
and better tasting than honey and
mother's milk, more delicious than
wine is this villain's blood!"

All who were close to him were
horrified. "This cannot be a man," they
thought. "This is a terrible demon,
a *rakshasa*!"

Bhima wiped his bloodstained lips,
gave a mocking laugh, and said, half
to himself: "That's you finished with.

You had a quick death." Then he took some of Duhshasana's blood in his cupped hands and called out to Duryodhana and the other Kurus: "See here, I am drinking your blood! I have sworn, and I have kept my oath!" And again he shouted victoriously.

His voice echoed across the field of the Kurus, making the flesh creep on all the warriors' backs. It was then that Karna first felt a great fear.

He tried to suppress it, to overcome his horror at Duhshasana's miserable death. He said to Shalya: "Drive me to Arjuna: now I feel like killing him!"

Arjuna, too, was seeking out Karna, anxious to fulfil the promise he had made to his brothers. Each searched for the other like a pair of venomous snakes, like two maddened elephants in the mating season, like two dark planets heading for a collision in the same orbit.

Karna asked Shalya: "What would you do if Arjuna were to kill me?"

"I should kill him," Shalya replied.

And Arjuna asked Krishna: "What would you do if Karna were to kill me?"

Krishna laughed, and said: "The sun will first fall from the heavens; the earth will break into pieces, and fire will burn with cold flames. But if it were to happen, it would mean that the end of the world was at hand. Then I would go and strangle him with my bare hands."

In that merciless combat, Karna discovered that Arjuna was no less a man than he. He drew from his quiver a specially made arrow, whose point was shaped like a snake's head, placed it in his bow, drew the string, and aimed at Arjuna's forehead.

"Not that arrow," Shalya told him. "Use another."

"I do not need another; I want this one," Karna snarled, irritated by Shalya's constant interference.

Krishna saw Karna's arrow with its snake's head swish through the air, leaving behind it a glowing trail, as straight as the parting in a girl's hair. He halted the team so suddenly that the horses fell to their knees. The arrow did not touch Arjuna, but only knocked off his splendid tiara, smashing it to tiny fragments of gold and precious stones.

The snake from the arrow crawled back to Karna, raised its head, and hissed: "Fire me again, and this time take better aim! Arjuna will die!"

"Who are you?" Karna asked.

"I am Arjuna's enemy. He killed my mother, and I am eager for vengeance. Shoot me, and you will be victorious."

"I never take the same arrow twice, even if I had to kill a hundred Arjunas," Karna retorted. "I do not need anyone's help. I have other weapons. Farewell, snake; go about your business."

Disappointed and angry, the snake

turned round, and tried to attack Arjuna.

"It is the snake whose mother was killed in the great fire in the forest of Khandava, when the god Agni ate his fill," Krishna explained. Arjuna fired six arrows at once, and that was the end of the snake.

Karna, eager to fight on, shouted insults at Arjuna, rounding on him rudely. But the god of time, Kala, saw that Karna's last hour was running out, and he whispered in his ear: "The earth wishes to swallow the left wheel of your chariot."

And indeed it was so: Karna's chariot began to lean over to the left. Karna scowled, and bitterly cursed his ill-fortune. He could not defend himself properly, since his chariot stood motionless, and Arjuna rode round him in ever-decreasing circles and harrassed him continually with his arrows. Karna jumped down and tried to release the wheel.

"Stop it, Arjuna!" he cried. "My left wheel is stuck! You know the rules of battle!"

"Remember other rules, Karna!" Krishna replied. "Do you recall how you insulted Draupadi? How Shakuni cheated at backgammon? How you refused to return the Pandus their kingdom when they came back from exile, though they had fulfilled all the conditions? Then and on many other occasions you did not pay much heed

to the rules, but happily ignored them."

Karna was stubbornly silent, endeavouring with both hands to raise the chariot and free the stuck wheel.

"Now!" Krishna told Arjuna. "Fire at him, before he climbs back into his chariot."

Arjuna picked out a heavy arrow with a broad point, drew his bow, and whispered: "Send him to the house of Yama, god of death!" And he loosed his grip on the arrow.

The string of his bow named *Gandiva* twanged mightily, and its echo rang through the heavens and the earth.

Karna's severed head, eyes wide open in horror, rolled along the ground, but his body, bleeding from many wounds, first stood up, and only then collapsed beside that fateful left chariot wheel.

King Shalya fled, and Arjuna, Krishna and all the Pandus blew their war shells. Karna's head with its pale face was reminiscent of a plucked white lotus blossom with a thousand petals; it was the head of a hero as bold as Indra of the thousand eyes, but now as dead as the thousand-rayed sun during the dark night.

Karna's death brought bitter disappointment and dark despair to the Kuru camp. All night long they held a council to decide what to do next, how to defeat the Pandu forces and kill the brothers.

"Let Shalya lead us now," proposed Ashwatthaman. "He is of a noble house, and few can match him in courage and skill at arms. Not only that, but he joined forces with us, even though the youngest Pandus, Nakula and Sahadeva, are the sons of his sister Madri."

"If you entrust me with a task, then I will fulfil it to the best of my ability and conscience," declared King Shalya, resolutely. "My riches, my kingdom and my life belong to the Kurus."

"Very well, my friend," Duryodhana pronounced, ceremoniously. "I request that you assume command of our army."

"Gladly," replied Shalya. "I think I know how to get the better of the Pandus, how to make them bleed."

When dawn broke on the eighteenth day of the great battle, the Kuru forces drew up in a formation ordered by their new general. The left wing was commanded by Kritavarman, of whom we shall hear more, and was made up of Trigartas from the north-west. On the right wing was Kripa, with the Shakas, the Persians and the Greeks. The rearguard was led by Ashwatthaman, with a force of Cambodians. In the

centre stood Duryodhana, with his most trusted warriors. It was a strong army, warlike and much more numerous than that of the Pandus, even though it did not have truth and justice on its side.

When the fighting broke out, it was as if the gods were clashing with those demons the *asuras,* so fierce was the struggle.

King Shalya, wishing to make an impression, attacked Yudhishthira straight away, showering him with light, feathered arrows. Yudhishthira fired off a heavy arrow with a broad point, bringing down Shalya's banner.

"Bhishma, Drona and Karna are dead," he cried, triumphantly. "That leaves Shalya, who shall die by my hand this day."

He picked up a long spear bound with gold and set with diamonds, and looked towards Shalya in order to judge the direction and distance. Whispering a spell to the spear, he drew back his arm, and hurled the weapon at Shalya. Shalya jumped up as if he

wished to catch the spear, like the flames of the sacrificial fire leaping out to lick the drops of ghee when the libation is made. But it slipped through his hands and buried itself deep in his chest. From his mouth, his nose and his ears gushed Shalya's crimson blood.

The Kuru soldiers dispersed like frightened merchants after the caravan's leader has been killed in a raid by bandits. Uncle Shakuni tried to hold them back, yelling: "Stop, you cowardly jackals! Forward! Into battle!" But it was to no avail.

Yudhishthira gave Sahadeva a fraternal pat on the back and said to him: "Do you see Shakuni? Take some horsemen and chariots and attack him.

Make sure you kill him; I will cover you."

Off Sahadeva rode. Shakuni threw a spear at him, but failed to hit his target. With a single arrow Sahadeva smashed Shakuni's bow in half, rendering it useless. Shakuni drew his sword, but another arrow from Sahadeva broke it into several pieces. Shakuni threw a heavy club at him, but Sahadeva had no trouble in warding it off with three arrows.

The Kuru soldiers who were supporting Shakuni ran away, and Shakuni, too, turned to make his escape.

Sahadeva rode after him, calling out: "Stop! Turn and fight, you coward! You cannot cheat in battle as you did in backgammon!"

Ashamed, Shakuni turned and raised his long lance. But Sahadeva broke it in half with a single arrow, and with two more severed both his arms. A fourth arrow with a broad gold tip beheaded Shakuni and all those foolish and shameful ideas which Kurus had used to try to harm the Pandus time after time died with him.

Sahadeva roared with delight. All the Pandus sounded a triumphant note on their war shells, and the Kuru forces began to withdraw. Duryodhana looked around the broad battlefield and saw only scattered groups of his own troops, and they were in retreat. Seized with despair and overcome by fear, with only a club in one hand he ran, so that no one might see him, to

a lake in the forest of Dwaitavana. In vain did Yudhishthira seek him on the battlefield to fight a duel with him; in vain did he look around and call Duryodhana's name.

But the Pandus had also suffered heavy losses. They were left with only ten thousand foot-soldiers, five thousand horsemen, two thousand chariots and seven hundred war elephants. That was not a great deal, for the battle had not yet been decided.

The triumphant shouts of the Pandus rang out over the whole of the Kurukshetra, reaching the camp of the Kurus. Kritavarman, Kripa and Ashwatthaman decided to go and find Duryodhana and discuss what to do now, since things could not go on as they were. After wandering about for a long time they finally found him.

Although they addressed him with civility, it was clear they resented his flight: "Come with us, Duryodhana; we must kill Yudhishthira. Our friends are dead. We must kill him, or die too."

"I am glad you have come," Duryodhana told them. "You can rest here, and refresh yourselves. Then we will be able to fight better. We are all tired. Tomorrow we will go into battle with new strength."

But Ashwatthaman did not agree. "No!" he cried. "Let us rise and go into battle at once! We are sure to win. We can win, but we must not sit around; we must fight while we are still able!"

While they were thus quarrelling, a group of hunters, who had daily been supplying Bhima with game and fish, arrived at the lake. They overheard the conversation of the four fugitives from the field of the Kurus, and said to themselves that they would slip quietly away and tell Bhima what they had

seen. They crept off nimbly, and ran to the Pandu camp.

Bhima rewarded them richly for their information, and went at once to Yudhishthira's tent. "They have run away to the lake in Dwaitavana forest!" he announced.

And the Pandus, tired though they were, hurried there at once.

Ashwatthaman was the first to hear the stamping of their feet and their heavy breathing. "They are coming!" he said. "I can hear them! We must go!"

"Then go," Duryodhana told them. "I will shelter here."

When the Pandus reached the lake, they could see no one. They looked around, combed the bushes and thickets, but could find no one.

After a while Yudhishthira laughed merrily, and said to his brothers: "Why are we searching for them, anyway? Let them crawl out of their hiding-places by themselves!" And he called out in a voice that carried right across the lake: "Why are you hiding, Duryodhana? Do you wish to save your miserable skin by cowardice? Crawl out of your hiding-place and fight! Where is your pride, you jackal who ran off with your tail between your legs!"

Duryodhana, hiding in the waters of the lake, replied: "I did not hide out

of fear. I have lost everything. My chariot has been smashed, my quivers are empty, my bow broken and my brothers killed. I need peace and quiet, for I am tired to death. You, too, are tired. Let us fight tomorrow."

"We are not tired, Duryodhana," Yudhishthira replied. "We have been after your blood for a long time now, and we do not wish to miss our chance. Come on out, come on out!"

"All that I fought for," Duryodhana cried dolefully, "is now lost. The whole world is like an old widow to me. All my friends are dead, and the world is as empty as a grainless husk. Take this world, and leave me in peace."

"You refused to give us what was ours by right, and now you would offer me the whole world? It is not yours to give! Come on out, Duryodhana, for you must be punished this very day."

"Very well: I will come out of hiding and fight," Duryodhana said. "But not with all of you at once, for that would not be honourable. I will fight you all, but one at a time. Then it will be an honourable fight."

"When all of you attacked Abhimanyu and killed him, was that an honourable fight?" shouted Yudhishthira. "But we are not like you. Choose which of us you wish to fight first, and I promise you that if you kill any one

of us five Pandu brothers, you may keep our kingdom for ever."

Duryodhana came out of his hiding-place and got ready to fight. Trying to hide his fear, he said: "I am ready. Which of you will be first?"

Krishna whispered to Yudhishthira: "It was not wise to offer your kingdom if he killed any one of you. What if he were to choose to fight Nakula or Sahadeva first? All the time you were in exile he practised with his club on an iron statue. Only Bhima can stand up to him, for he has immense strength. But Duryodhana is clever, too. I think you are again tempting providence, as when you lost everything to Shakuni."

Yudhishthira was shamefaced and silent.

"I will fight him first and last," said Bhima, stepping forward, "for I will kill him outright." And he shouted to Duryodhana: "On guard!"

With slow, heavy steps, Bhima drew closer to Duryodhana. "Remember all the evil you have done us, and prepare to die," he said.

"You speak too much," Duryodhana retorted. "Here you have me: fight, and fight honourably!"

They leapt for each other like a pair of angry lions. Their clubs struck a cloud of sparks from each other like a swarm of fireflies fleeing from a bat.

Bhima and Duryodhana lunged at each other, dodged, swung round and jumped about like mountain bears attacked by wild bees; they stood waiting, then suddenly leapt forward, trying to outwit and out-manoeuvre each other and strike a fatal blow. Now

Duryodhana managed to strike Bhima on the kneecap. Bhima yelled like a wounded panther, swung his club, and struck Duryodhana on the thigh. Duryodhana staggered, and even fell to his knees, but he was soon up again and struck Bhima on the head. Bhima stood as firm as a mountain peak in a storm, and blood trickled down his temples. Then he suddenly swung his club, and Duryodhana went down like a felled dammar tree. The Pandus hooted with delight.

But Duryodhana recovered himself instantly; he rose like an elephant climbing out of a lake after its morning bath, and struck Bhima in the chest with such force that he tore off his rhinoceros skin breastplate and his shirt of mail. For a moment Bhima stood motionless, as if he had lost consciousness. But then he took hold of his club with both hands, swung it back, and with a roar like thunder smashed it across Duryodhana's legs with such force that he broke both his thighbones.

Duryodhana fell, and the ground shook. Trees and rocks shuddered, and from the depths of the mountains a dark rumbling was heard. Rivers flowed backwards, and lightning struck from a clear sky. Blood appeared in the wells, and headless monsters with many arms and legs danced all around. Bhima gave a roar of triumph.

"You laughed when you humiliated and insulted Draupadi," Bhima said to Duryodhana. "Now you may laugh at yourself, at what you have come to!" And he kicked Duryodhana in the head.

"No, Bhima," Yudhishthira reproached him. "Do not strike a man when he is down. He is a king, and our cousin. Now he has nothing — he has lost everything. He deserves pity more than anything."

Bhima stood in front of Yudhishthira and honoured him as his eldest brother. "It is all over, brother. All the thorns have been removed from our heels," he added, joyfully. "What belongs to us by right is ours again."

"The great struggle is over," said Yudhishthira, but there was a touch of sadness and regret along with the joy in his voice. "Duryodhana will harm us no more. With Krishna's help we have been victorious."

"Let us go," Krishna said. "There is nothing to keep us here. This villain," and he pointed a finger at Duryodhana, "can stay here. He deserves no better."

The Pandus blew on their war shells, and left the miserable Duryodhana dying on the banks of the lake in the Dwaitavana forest.

First of all they went to the Kuru camp, where they exercised their right as victors and took all the precious objects. Their booty was a rich one: gold, silver, pearls, jewels, embroidered hangings, and rare skins and furs. In a merry mood they went back to their own camp, after which they performed the cleansing ritual in the waves of the River Oghavati.

Krishna and his company left for Hastinapura to comfort the blind old King Dhritarashtra and his Queen, Gandhari, who had lost all their sons in the great battle. The five Pandu brothers rode to Indraprastha, where their faithful wife Draupadi and their mother Kunti were waiting for them.

Duryodhana, his hair matted and his body covered in dust, sweat and dried blood, lay helpless on the bank of the lake, waiting for death. He looked around him, hissing like a cobra about to strike.

Duryodhana's counsellor and charioteer, Sanyjaya, who had told the blind king all that was going in the great battle, since the wise holy man Vyasa had given him the power of miraculous vision, left Hastinapura with the king's permission, and hurried

to the side of the mortally wounded Duryodhana.

Duryodhana greeted him with a casual nod of his head, and said: "Sanyjaya, tell my parents that when I was lying here with my legs broken, Bhima kicked me in the head so that he might humiliate me still further. Tell them also, that I have always performed the proper ceremonies, sacrifices and libations, and that I have been kind to those I considered worthy of my favour. I studied the principles of the three planes of being, read the holy *Vedas*, and rode only on pedigree horses. Now, as I am preparing to leave this wretched world, I am happy.

I am leaving to join Bhishma, Drona, Karna and the other bold warriors who laid down their lives in the great struggle."

Sanyjaya told all this to King Dhritarashtra and Queen Gandhari in Hastinapura.

When the sun began to sink in the west, Kritavarman, Kripa and Ashwatthaman came out of their hiding-places and met on the banks of the lake beside the dying Duryodhana, who lay there as miserable as the clear moon fallen into a swamp.

Ashwatthaman cried in amazement: "You — lying here wounded! Truly is it written that all things pass

away, and nothing is left behind."

"Death awaits all of us," said Duryo-dhana, wiping his eyes. "It is the will of Brahma. It is all up with me, but do not pity me or grieve for me. I fought well, as did all of you."

Ashwatthaman took his hand and said with emotion: "I promise you by all that is dear to me; I promise by the highest truth of all, that this night I will kill all the Pandus. Tell me I may do it, master!"

Duryodhana revived a little, for Ashwatthaman's words had warmed

his heart. He said to Kripa: "Pass me that jug of water."

He took the jug in his right hand, sprinkled water on Ashwatthaman's head, and said to him in a voice which was already weak: "Ashwatthaman, I make you commander of the Kuru army, however its might may be diminished."

Duryodhana embraced the new commander, and Ashwatthaman, Kripa and Kritavarman vanished in the twilight. Then Duryodhana died calmly and quietly, though it took a long time.

Furious Vengeance

Soon after the sun set, the three conspirators crept up to the Pandu camp and hid in a nearby grove. Voices and shouts could be heard from the camp, and Ashwatthaman was afraid they had been spotted and that the Pandus were preparing to find and kill them, so they moved deeper into the thick forest. Tormented by hatred, a longing for vengeance, and a terrible thirst, they lay down to rest. Kripa and Kritavarman fell asleep at once, but Ashwatthaman could not sleep a wink.

He woke his two companions and told them of his plan. They were not as enthusiastic as Ashwatthaman had expected.

Kripa said: "The life of a man is governed by two forces, fate and character. If they are in harmony, he enjoys success. One man grasps his opportunity, while another lets it slip through his fingers. I must admit I do not know what to do. And he who does not know, should take advice. Let us go and ask Dhritarashtra, Gandhari and Vidura; they will surely advise us well."

Ashwatthaman listened to this with displeasure. "Different people have different ideas," he said, emphatically. "But each is convinced that his are the right ones. You must decide for yourselves, but tonight *I* am going to kill the sleeping Pandus and their allies. Thus I will do my duty, and I will be happy."

"I see you are filled with a desire for vengeance," noted Kripa, "and that perhaps not even the king of the gods, Indra himself, could dissuade you. But I should advise you to lay down your arms and get a good night's sleep. In the morning we will both go with you."

"How can I sleep," snapped Ashwatthaman, his eyes fiery with rage, "when I am so angry? I will sleep long and

deep as soon as my enemies are dead!"
And he stood up briskly and made as if
to leave.

"Wait! Where are you going?" Kritavarman asked him. "Did we not say we
would go with you in the morning?"

"I want to kill Dhrishtadyumna. If
he dies without a weapon in his hands,
he will not get to the paradise of warriors — that is what I want!" Ashwatthaman explained. "Come with me
now!"

Kripa and Kritavarman allowed
themselves to be persuaded, and they
set off with Ashwatthaman towards the
Pandu camp. They walked quietly,
without speaking, ready to kill all who
crossed their path.

Everything was quiet; the Pandu
army was asleep, soothed by the sweet
knowledge that the great battle was
won. They had not set many sentries.

When Ashwatthaman, Kripa and
Kritavarman reached the camp, they

suddenly saw a huge and fearful figure standing at the gate. The terrible monster was dressed in a tiger skin; across his left shoulder and his right side a long, mottled snake was curled, in his hands he held murderous weapons, and flames shot from his mouth. Ashwatthaman shot several arrows at him, but the monster swallowed them as if they had been sweetmeats. Then he threw a heavy spear, but it burned up in the flames of the monster's fiery breath like a blade of dry grass. Then Ashwatthaman thrust his double-edged sword into the creature — and it slipped from his hand and vanished in the monster's belly like a mongoose in its lair! And the monster just stood there, rolling its eyes and breathing fire.

"This is strange — incredible," thought Ashwatthaman. "Only Shiva himself can help me here, or I am lost." And he began at once to call upon the mighty god Shiva:

"Shiva, great god who
Is also known as Hara,
I beg your protection,
Dread lord of the universe!
Shiva, god with the blue throat,
You have a necklace of skulls,

Three eyes in your head;
You ride on the bull Nandin,
Your spouse is the divine Kali,
Called Parvati and Durga.
Shiva, help me now,
Save me from all danger!"

At that moment the monster disappeared, and instead of it there stood
Shiva, his famous sword glinting in his
hand. He gave a thunderous laugh and
said: "I will help you, Ashwatthaman!"
And he and his sword entered Ashwatthaman's body. Suddenly, Ashwatthaman felt an immense strength, and he
was more belligerent than ever. A company of the *rakshasa* demons took their
place by his side. Kripa and Kritavarman stayed to keep watch.

"Stand here and kill all who try
to escape," Ashwatthaman told them.
"I will pass through the camp like the
terrible shadow of the god of death and
destruction, Yama."

And he and the frenzied *rakshasas*
entered the Pandu camp.

In the first great tent the Panchalas'
soldiers slept. On a bed with silken
covers lay Draupadi's brother, Dhrish-

tadyumna. Ashwatthaman went up to him and kicked him roughly. Dhrishtadyumna was awake in an instant; when he saw his enemy he stiffened. Ashwatthaman caught him by the hair, dragged him from his bed, and knocked him to the ground. Half asleep, Dhrishtadyumna was scarcely able to defend himself. Ashwatthaman struck him in the throat, and kicked him in the chest.

"Kill me quickly," croaked Dhrishtadyumna, "but let me die with a weapon in my hand. Let me die a warrior's death!"

"He who has slain his guru does not deserve to enter paradise," snarled Ashwatthaman, softly. And he went on kicking him in the groin and stomach until Dhrishtadyumna gave up.

Those who tried to escape were killed by Kripa and Kritavarman, who set fire to the camp from three sides. Amid the flames Ashwatthaman ran back and forth, beheading and dismembering with his sword all he met, in which he was greatly assisted by Shiva's *rakshasas*.

When the dawn drew near, the *rakshasas* vanished, and Ashwatthaman, tired and splattered with blood, left the Pandu camp. He held his sword so firmly it seemed to be fused to his arm as a single deadly weapon.

Smiling at Kripa and Kritavarman, he said: "The Panchalas and Draupadi's sons and brother are dead. The Matsyas and the Somakas, too, are slain. Come, we will tell Duryodhana; he will be pleased."

On the banks of the lake in the forest of Dwaitavana, Duryodhana was still alive; but his breath was getting short, and he was vomiting blood; jackals lay in wait nearby, and the vultures and buzzards circled impatiently above.

"Duryodhana is close to death," said Kripa. "He who was once surrounded by holy men and sages is now attended only by carnivorous creatures. Such are the twists of fate."

"If you are still alive, and can hear us, Duryodhana," Ashwatthaman addressed him, "then know you that of our enemies only the five Pandu brothers, Krishna and his charioteer Satyaki are still alive. Dhrishtadyumna is dead, as are his sons, and none of Draupadi's sons is left alive. The Pandus have no sons, and therefore they will be cursed through the ages."

"What you tell me," whispered Duryodhana, "is as a cool breeze to my fiery brow. You have achieved what Bhishma, Karna and Drona could not. Live in happiness, and may you be successful in all things, Ashwatthaman! We shall meet in heaven."

And he breathed his last.

Only a few were lucky enough to escape Ashwatthaman's demented slaughter at the Pandu camp. One of them was Dhrishtadyumna's charioteer, who managed to get away under cover of darkness, and early the next morning reached Yudhishthira to inform him of the disaster which had befallen the sleeping Pandu forces at the Kurukshetra.

Yudhishthira, though a brave and hardened man, wept bitterly. "We defeated them, and they have destroyed us. We are like those merchants who safely crossed the wide ocean, only to drown in the river close to their home city."

He climbed into his chariot and hurried to the Kurukshetra. There he saw his sons, nephews and friends, his soldiers and his hired mercenaries, all either dead or dying.

Before long Draupadi, too, arrived. Her clear eyes were clouded with grief, as when the sun's face is hidden by an eclipse. She took one look at the devastation, and fainted. Yudhishthira brought her round, raised her to her feet, and embraced her kindly. Draupadi grieved deeply.

"Avenge them; avenge all these dead, murdered in their sleep!" she moaned. "You must kill Ashwatthaman!"

"They say Ashwatthaman has fled somewhere into the forest, where he is hiding," said Yudhishthira.

"I once heard," Draupadi recalled, "that Ashwatthaman was born with a jewel on his skull. Kill him, and bring me that stone!"

By now the other Pandu brothers had arrived at the Kurukshetra, and they were cruelly affected by what they saw.

"Let us all go to the wise priest, Vyasa," said Arjuna. And they drove to the banks of the holy River Ganges, until they reached the forest hermitage where the holy Vyasa sat, dressed only in blades of sacred grass, and surrounded by his disciples. Among them the Pandus spotted Ashwatthaman. What a surprise that was, on both sides!

Bhima grabbed his bow and cried: "Leave him to me! He is mine!"

Ashwatthaman sensed that his last hour had come, and remembered the magic formula once revealed to him by his father, Drona. Picking a long, thin blade of grass, he used his magic *mantra* to turn it into a deadly weapon. "Let this weapon destroy the Pandus!" he thought.

But Bhima foresaw Ashwatthaman's intentions, and said to Arjuna: "Shoot with that weapon against weapons which Drona once gave you!"

Arjuna deftly grasped his mighty weapon against weapons, and thought: "Let this weapon against weapons destroy Ashwatthaman's weapon!"

And since all this happened in a single instant, no sooner had the terrible flame shot from Ashwatthaman's weapon, than a shot from Arjuna's weapon against weapons struck that flame, exploding with a terrible din

and sending the flame flying; it did not disappear from the world, however, but flew through the air seeking a target. The earth shook, the mountains and cliffs shuddered, trees were uprooted, rivers changed course and flowed in a quite different direction, lakes overflowed their banks, and shooting stars fell from the sky. Only the action of two great holy men, Vyasa and Narada, prevented the destruction of all three worlds, and of the whole of the universe.

"What unheard-of madness is this?" Vyasa called out to them, passionately. "Have you lost all prudence and wisdom? Why do you use such inhuman weapons of doom?"

Arjuna said in his defence: "I saw that Ashwatthaman wished to destroy us. We had to defend ourselves. Tell us, then, what we are to do."

Vyasa told Ashwatthaman: "You must admit that Arjuna did not seek to kill you, but fired in self-defence. There has been enough fighting; now you must stop! Enough human lives have been destroyed. The Pandus will live, and you will give them the precious stone from your head."

"This jewel," objected Ashwatthaman, "means more to me than all the treasures concealed in the bowels of the earth. He who has it is protected from all weapons, from disease and from hunger. I should never give it to anyone, but since you, whom I honour, ask it of me, I will give it to the Pandus." And he handed the jewel to Vyasa.

"But my destructive flame is wandering through space, and has yet to find a target," added Ashwatthaman. "It must find one, or it will destroy the whole world. Let it enter the wombs of the Pandu women."

"Very well," Vyasa agreed. "Let it enter their wombs, if you will; but that must be the end of the matter."

Then Krishna spoke, and said to Ashwatthaman with a smile: "When Virata's daughter Uttara married Abhimanyu and became Arjuna's daughter-in-law, a certain holy man of the Brahman caste prophesied to her that when the house of the Pandus died out, a son, Parikshit, would be born to her."

"Then my flame shall destroy Parikshit also," snapped Ashwatthaman, angrily.

"It will not," Krishna told him. "Parikshit will become a famous king, and your flame will long have been extinguished. But you have sent your flame of destruction into the wombs of the Pandu women; therefore you are the murderer of unborn children. I must punish you, and will punish you gladly, and as you deserve. For three thousand years you will walk this world alone and abandoned, without a single friend and without a wife, and no one shall speak to you. You will stink foully of pus and decomposing blood, and will

have to hide in solitary, swampy forests. And throughout that period you will be tormented by every disease which affects man and animals, though you will be unable to die."

Ashwatthaman bowed his head and quietly slipped into the deep forest, and no one ever saw him again.

The wise holy man Vyasa gave Ashwatthaman's jewel to Yudhishthira, who went with the Pandus and Krishna to Draupadi, lest she should worry over their absence.

When Yudhishthira gave her Ashwatthaman's stone, she smiled and said: "I wanted only vengeance, and I thank you and all your friends. I should like you to wear the jewel, and may it bring you luck!"

Yudhishthira placed the stone on his head, where it shone like a bright full moon at a mountain top, on a pleasantly cool autumn night.

When Yudhishthira heard that his uncle Dhritarashtra had left Hastinapura to visit the Kurukshetra, he went there with his brothers to meet him; Draupadi went with them, with the noble Krishna and Dhritarashtra's bastard son Yuyutsu.

When the Kuru women, who were mourning their dead on the field of the Kurus, saw Yudhishthira, they wept more than ever, wringing their hands and berating him in their desperate grief for what had happened in the

great battle. Yudhishthira took no notice of them. What else could he do? He had to ignore them, for there is no good answer for those who blame you when the battle is over.

He went up to King Dhritarashtra, greeted him respectfully, and wiped the dust from his feet. The other Pandus did the same. Reluctantly, Dhritarashtra embraced Yudhishthira, the eldest of the Pandu brothers. But when he came to the mighty Bhima, his anger and hatred, nourished by his deep sorrow, erupted. The divine Krishna foresaw what he intended to do, and pushed Bhima aside, thrusting instead into Dhritarashtra's open arms an iron statue.

King Dhritarashtra embraced Bhima's statue with the strength of ten thousand elephants, and the statue was turned to dust. But the effort weakened the old king greatly. He slumped to his knees like a spreading cow-wheat, whose branches are unable to support the load of so many dark red flowers, and coughed blood.

The faithful Sanyjaya helped him up, and said to him quietly: "Sire, this is not fitting."

Dhritarashtra's wrath subsided, to be replaced by regret, and the blind old king wept: "Oh, Bhima, alas! What have I done?"

Krishna placed a hand on his shoulder and said: "Do not lament, Dhritarashtra, do not grieve. You have

crushed only an iron statue of Bhima. But tell me: would it have helped to kill Bhima? Would it have restored your fallen sons to life?"

Dhritarashtra had no answer to that. Servant girls ran up and washed the old king.

But Krishna went on: "Sire, you are old, and know well all that is contained in the holy writings. You know the ancient traditions and the laws. Why do you nurture such wrath and hatred, when it must be clear to you that all that happened during the great struggle is nothing more than the result of your own foolish weakness towards your own sons, especially towards Duryo-dhana, whom you were not able to persuade or control?"

King Dhritarashtra nodded his head sadly, and replied: "You are right, Krishna. I was too fond of my sons, and forgot the laws of the moral order. You did well to push Bhima aside from my embrace. My wrath and hatred have already died down. Allow me now to embrace all the younger

Pandus, for my own sons are all dead; now my whole happiness lies in my nephews."

And the old king tearfully embraced Bhima, Arjuna and the twins Nakula and Sahadeva, and blessed them.

Then the Pandus turned to Queen Gandhari. They greeted her respectfully, as if she were their own mother. The unhappy Gandhari, mother of a hundred sons, of whom none now remained, wished in her despair to curse Yudhishthira, whom she considered the cause of all her woes. It is not uncommon for the loving heart of a mother to cease to distinguish good and evil, right and wrong, and to measure her own children only with immense love and kindness, which blind all the senses.

The holy sage Vyasa, in his endless wisdom, foresaw Queen Gandhari's ungenerous intention, and with the speed of thought appeared in front of her. He said: "Now is not the time for cursing, my dear daughter-in-law! Lay aside your anger, for peace is more important."

Gandhari replied: "I do not wish the Pandus any evil. I do not want them to die. But my heart bitterly regrets the death of my sons. There is one thing I cannot forget: in Krishna's presence, Bhima struck Duryodhana, my eldest son, below the belt with his club, and caused him mortal injury in combat. That makes me very sad."

Then Bhima stepped forward and said: "One way or the other, I did what I had to. It was him, or me. Forgive me,

Gandhari, if you can. No one would have been able to overcome Duryodhana in a duel fought exactly according to the rules; I had to use a trick against him. But Duryodhana did not always deal fairly with us, either; there are many examples of this, and you surely know of them yourself."

"I daresay you are right," answered Gandhari. "And I am glad to hear you praise Duryodhana's skill in battle. He surely deserved a more dignified death, but what has happened, has happened. Nevertheless, on the field of battle you drank Duhshasana's blood! What could be more horrible? Are you not ashamed, Bhima?"

"It seemed like that," Bhima admitted, "but Duhshasana's blood did not pass my lips and teeth. Karna would witness that I was bloodied only on my hands and lips. You surely remember what I vowed when your sons insulted Draupadi in the gaming room. And if I were not to keep my vow, I should lose my honour as a Kshatriya. That is why I did what I did. Do not blame only us Pandus for everything! Do not your sons, especially Duryodhana and Duhshasana, bear part of the blame — in my view the greater part of it?"

"But you have killed the hundred sons of an old, blind king! Could you not have spared one at least — perhaps the youngest, weakest, who harmed you the least?" Again Gandhari's anger flared. "Where is the eldest of the Pandus? Where is Yudhishthira?"

"I am here," Yudhishthira said, and came before Queen Gandhari. "Yes, I am the cause of it all. I deserve your

curse. Then curse me!" He spoke proudly, and stood firmly in front of the queen, but he was afraid, none the less.

Queen Gandhari only sighed, and was silent. Yudhishthira bowed humbly, and wiped the dust from the queen's feet. Gandhari, though she had her eyes bound, out of love and honour for her blind husband, looked from beneath the bandage at Yudhishthira's feet as he bowed to her, and at that moment ugly, septic blisters appeared on his feet. The other Pandus were anxious, and fidgeted nervously.

But Queen Gandhari had already forgotten her anger, and spoke cordially and kindly to the Pandus. Only their dolorous mother, Kunti, seeing her

sons for the first time in many years, covered her face with a corner of her sari and wept quietly, overcome with happiness, grief and regret. The faithful and loving Draupadi also wept, lamenting the loss of her slaughtered sons. "What am I to do with a kingdom," she moaned, "when my sons have fallen in battle?"

Queen Gandhari embraced her and said: "Do not grieve, daughter, do not grieve! What is the point of it all? My sorrow is greater. But such are the times we live in. What can we women do against the belligerency which possesses our menfolk?"

All around them, across the broad Kurukshetra, lay the bloodied and disfigured bodies of the fallen warriors of the Kuru and Pandu armies. Everywhere they looked there were fallen brothers, sons, fathers, husbands and other relatives, as well as hired mercenaries, who were no less dead than the rest. Among the bodies wolves and jackals ran, and buzzards and vultures feasted on them. It was a scene of destruction and doom. The countryside was full of evil spirits, *pishachas* and *rakshasas,* and they enjoyed nightly feasts of food and drink.

Those who now stood on that bloody battlefield and looked at the devastation caused by the great fratricidal struggle, did not feel well. Some froze to the spot in horror, while others fainted, and others went to one side and vomited discreetly.

When Gandhari saw the body of her

eldest son, Duryodhana, lying by the banks of the lake, she fell into a faint as if she had been struck down by a Himalayan pine. It was a long time before she came round again. She arranged her hair, wiped her eyes, and in anger and maternal despair said to Krishna:

"Why, O Krishna, did you allow
The members of our two
Related families to
Slay each other willy-nilly?
Why did you foolishly refrain
From warning against this
Fratricidal struggle, you who
Speak so eloquently?
I am, noble Krishna,
An obedient and faithful wife,
Mother of a hundred dead sons.
So I now curse you thus:
For six and thirty years you
Shall be a cause of doom
For all your faithful kinsfolk,
To your eternal shame!"

The noble Krishna only smiled: "Your curse does not frighten me. No one, not even the gods themselves, can slay the house of Yadua. Only I myself can do that, and your curse will help me do that which I have in mind. But why do you curse me? A Brahman mother teaches her sons to perform ceremonies, sacrifices and libations. A cow has her calves to bear the yoke, and to give milk. The Shudra women teach their children to serve the higher castes, and a Vaishyu mother knows her children will devote themselves to agriculture or to trade. But a Kshatriya mother such as you must know that her sons are warriors, and warriors fall in battle. Why are you surprised at that? Why are you lamenting? That is how things have to be."

"I suppose it cannot be otherwise," whispered Gandhari; she bowed her head, and wept quietly.

King Dhritarashtra said: "It is time for us to burn the bodies of the dead with due ceremony, for the salvation of one whose body is eaten by the jackals or the vultures is threatened."

Then Yudhishthira gave instructions to the sacrificial priest of the Kurus, Sudharman, and that of the Pandus, Dhaumaya, to begin preparations for a great funeral. "Make ready plenty of sandal and aloe woods, and fragrant ointments and oils," he told them. "None of the dead must be deprived of his last honours."

Sanyjaya, Vidura and Yuyutsu were put at the disposal of Dhaumaya and Sudharman, and it was not long before the flames of a huge funeral pyre

licked upwards, in which ended the pilgrimage through life of many a valiant warrior.

Yudhishthira sat on a magnificent and splendid throne, facing the east. On one side of him sat Krishna and Satyaki, on the other Bhima and Arjuna; a little below them, on ivory stools inlaid with gold, sat the youngest of the Pandus, Nakula and Sahadeva. Opposite Yudhishthira the old, blind King Dhritarashtra was enthroned, with Yuyutsu, Vidura, Sanyjaya and Queen Gandhari. They were preparing for the great ceremony where Yudhishthira would be made king by sprinkling with water. For the royal crown is the outward symbol of sovereign power, but the sprinkling on the king's head of holy water from the Ganges is a lasting symbol, an eternal, inalienable seal on his kingship.

Everything needed for the great ceremony was ready: white flowers, the holy *swastika,* soil from the bowels of mother earth, gold, silver, precious stones, pearls and corals. Yudhishthira's subjects, with the priests and holy men at their head, brought golden jugs of water, silver and copper vessels, two-handled pots, garlands of flowers, toasted rice from the autumn harvest, bales of holy grass, cow's milk, honey, ghee, fragrant wood for the sacred fire, and gold-decorated shells, whose long-drawn-out sound was to add to the grandeur of the occasion.

The Pandu priest, Dhaumaya, had built according to Krishna's plans an altar facing north-east. Yudhishthira and Draupadi sat down on the tiger skin called the *Sarwatabhadra,* and the priest Dhaumaya began to recite the Vedic *mantras* and to drip ghee into the sacred fire. Then he picked up a sea shell in both his hands and sprinkled Yudhishthira's head with the holy water of the River Ganges, which was the heavenly aspergation. Then old Dhritarashtra sprinkled Yudhishthira, which was the earthly one.

After this ceremony, another was held in Yudhishthira's name for those killed in the great battle. When all the ceremonies were over, all the subjects, citizens, villagers, holy men and penitents, and those who came to represent the wild tribes of the mountains and forests, were richly entertained and plied with gifts.

The Pandus, too, went to celebrate, and to rest. Yudhishthira stayed in Dhritarashtra's palace. His brothers took up residence in the palaces of the eldest Kurus, as Yudhishthira instructed them: Bhima in the palace of Duryodhana, Arjuna in that of Duhshasana, and the twins Nakula and Sahadeva in the palaces of Durmarshana and Durmukha.

In these palaces they found the softest beds, beautiful and affectionate girls with dark eyes the shape of almonds and the petals of lotus flowers, excellent dishes with tastily spiced sauces, and the most delicious of wines. For their entertainment there were the pick of the most able musicians, playing all manner of instruments, and singers of renown; the skill of these entertainers almost outshone that of the heavenly *gandharvas* themselves. The Pandus spent the evening and night in merrymaking, which was a comfort to them after the hardships and tribulations of exile and of the great battle, for the wheels of time and fate roll on without hesitation; it is the only thing in the universe which has neither beginning nor end, which never came into being and will never cease to be.

The next morning all the Pandu brothers went to visit Krishna, who, dressed in yellow, was sitting on a golden throne adorned with emeralds, rubies

and pearls. On his breast shone a splendid brooch with thirteen jewels; it was the *Kaushtubha,* which came out of the ocean when it was struck by the gods and the *asuras.*

It was such a magnificent piece of jewellery that it cannot be described in human language, since any comparison would be inadequate and unfitting. It was something beyond imagination, something immensely dazzling and indescribable. Yet this jewel was like the moon veiled in cloud, for it was outshone by the glow of the noble Krishna.

Krishna sat in deep meditation, and did not even notice the arrival of the Pandus.

Yudhishthira addressed him thus: "You are as calm and as firm as a cliff standing over the wild rapids, as steady as the flame of a closed lantern. I bow before you, Krishna, who dissolves all doubt." And all the Pandus bowed courteously.

Krishna awoke from his meditation, smiled, and said: "Welcome. I am glad you have come. I have just seen old Bhishma, who is lying on his bed of arrows like a dying fire on a bed of ruddy ashes. He is thinking of me. I beg you, Yudhishthira, go to him and ask him

all that concerns the four senses of being, the customs and ceremonies, the four social castes and the four seasons of life; ask him, too, about the duties of a monarch. For when Bhishma dies the source of all knowledge and science will dry up. Go at once, Yudhishthira, and go quickly!"

"I will gladly go, together with my brothers," Yudhishthira replied. "But come with us."

Krishna assented, and told his charioteer Satyaki to prepare his chariot and harness the team.

And they drove to the place where Bhishma still lay, shot through with arrows, like the sun fallen to earth. They drove alone, without an escort of soldiers, for Yudhishthira had said that where grave matters are discussed seriously there should not be too many people present.

When they arrived, they greeted Bhishma with due respect, and looked on him with humble regret.

Krishna asked him: "Bhishma, wise and eloquent Bhishma, is your mind as clear as it used to be? Your father Shantanu gave you a gift that no one in the world possesses, not even I — that you will die only when you wish to yourself. Who else, therefore, can tell us of the everlasting truths of life which run through the past, the present and the future? Please answer the questions which are tormenting us."

"I welcome and greet you, Krishna,"
said Bhishma, softly. "And I welcome and greet the Pandu brothers. The arrows with which I am pierced burn me inside like poison, and outside like fire. But in your presence it is as if all the pain had receded. How can a pupil like myself tell a teacher such as you anything new?"

"Worthy and noble Bhishma," Krishna said. "You might teach the gods themselves. Do as we ask, and fulfil our humble request." And he placed his hand on Bhishma's brow, wet with the cold sweat of death.

"Suddenly the searing pain is gone, and the fever that contorts the mind," Bhishma told him. "It is surely because of your kindness, Krishna. Now I can clearly see the past, present and future; I can see them as clearly as the fingers on the hand I have in front of my face."

"That is good, Bhishma," said Krishna. "Yudhishthira would like to ask you something, but he is afraid you will curse him. He feels guilty for the great struggle, and for the murder of kinfolk."

"Let him lay aside his fear; he has no need to be afraid. The duties of a Kshatriya warrior and the laws of war state that one must kill all who are on the other side, no matter who they might be."

Shyly, Yudhishthira came forward to Bhishma, and gently touched his foot by way of greeting.

"Wise men say," he addressed him, bashfully, "that the duties of a king are the gravest duties of all. What does that mean? What are those duties?"

And Bhishma told him: "Above all, a king must not lose his heart, that is courage and kindness. He must not allow anything evil or wrong to take place. If a king is dedicated to truth and constantly defends it, he need not be dedicated to anything else. Truth, right and justice are the highest duties of a king. Solicitation for his subjects, care of them and of their well-being — those are the duties of a king. The ancient law-giver Manu says:

'Like a boat with a hole in the bottom,
Avoid, if only you can:
The teacher who is silent,
The priest who does not know holy writ,

The king who does not care for his
people,
The wife with a slit mouth
The herdsman who lounges about the
village,
And the barber who goes wandering.'

The duty of a king is to work, care,
govern and take decisions. A king
knows no rest. A king who does not
work, act and decide, is as useless as
a snake without venom. And a king
must always be watchful and wary, and
must know all that is going on. Even
the weakest and most inconsequential
individual, if he becomes an enemy,
can bring about destruction, just as
a tiny spark can light a fire in a great
forest."

"And what are the duties of the four
castes?" Yudhishthira continued.

"It is laid down that the Brahmans
shall devote themselves to learning,
teaching, making sacrifices and libations on their own behalf and on that
of others, distributing gifts and receiving them," Bhishma said. "The Kshatriyas are to devote themselves to learning, making sacrifices and libations,
distributing gifts, gaining what is necessary for living by means of battle, and
protecting living creatures. The Vaish-
yus are to learn, make sacrifices and
libations, distribute gifts, till the soil,
rear animals, ply the better trades, or
be merchants. The Shudras are to be
obedient and disciplined towards the

higher castes, to work as servants, to take the less noble trades and to be actors and jugglers."

"How can a sovereign who wishes for victory wage a war without breaking the moral code?" asked Yudhishthira.

"A king can use two methods, the direct or the indirect. If he is the first to attack, this is the direct method; if he is attacked and defends himself, this is the indirect method. Set a thief to catch a thief: the best weapon against treachery is treachery."

"Which duties are the highest, good Bhishma? Which are the most meritorious in this life, and in the lives to come?"

"The highest duty of all is to honour one's mother, father and guru. That which they teach you to do becomes your task, and you must fulfil it, come what may. Mother, father and guru are like the three holy fires at the great sacrifice. A guru is worth ten learned Brahmans, but a father is worth ten gurus. A mother is worth ten fathers; indeed, she is worth more than the whole world. Thus spoke the ancient sages. But in my view a just guru is worth more than mother or father, for these two formed our body only, whereas a guru forms and guides our immortal soul."

"Sometimes it is impossible to distinguish between truth and lie," said Yudhishthira. "What is truth, and what is a lie? When is it right to lie?"

"Truth is what is in keeping with the moral order," Bhishma replied. "Nothing is higher than truth. But there is little of it in this world of ours. You should never tell the truth if it would hide a lie, and it is good to lie if this supports the truth."

Bhishma's strength faded, and he fell silent. Krishna and the Pandu brothers withdrew to a distance, so that their speech should not disturb him.

"It is clear that of the four senses of life the foremost is salvation," said Yudhishthira. "But what of the other three? Which of them is the foremost?"

"The moral order," replied Vidura, a wise and prudent old man, without hesitation, "because the other two, profit and delight, depend upon it."

"I disagree," said Arjuna, "for profit is the result of action; a lazy man can achieve nothing. Therefore I would put profit in first place."

But Bhima said: "I cannot agree! Delight and lust are the main things, since without desire and effort neither profit, nor morality can be achieved, let alone salvation."

"Your opinion has something to be said for it," admitted Yudhishthira. "But who in the world can decide and act according to his desire? I myself decide and act only as my fate leads me to. My aim in life is salvation. And morality, profit and desire are merely three ways of achieving that."

Bhishma had recovered from his faint, and Yudhishthira asked him: "Bhishma, good Bhishma, how is a man to choose a friend?"

"He should choose one who is not selfish," Bhishma told him, "nor intolerant, dishonourable or perfidious, suspicious or good-for-nothing; nor should he neglect his duty, or what his guru tells him, and he should not be a liar, or godless or a gambler."

"Now tell me of the duties of a man in the four seasons of life," Yudhishthira requested.

"It is for a pupil to learn, to keep the sacred fire burning, to perform the ceremony of cleansing, take the vow of poverty, and be at the disposal of his guru until his death," Bhishma told him. "A husbandman should acquire his needs by the work appropriate to his station, marry a girl of the same caste, but not a relation, give gifts to the gods, dead ancestors, guests and servants. A hermit should sleep on the ground, plait a pigtail, dress in antelope skin, maintain a sacrificial fire, perform' the ceremony of cleansing, honour the gods and his ancestors, and live on the food offered by the forest. A wandering penitent should tame his senses, not perform any deeds, have no property, avoid contact with people, accept only alms, skirt around inhabited places, live in the desert and maintain internal and external cleanliness."

"And how is a good man to behave, Bhishma?"

"He should behave morally, assiduously and with restraint. He should not defecate in the street, in cattle pens or in rice fields. He should not urinate with his face towards the sun, nor lie in his bed after dawn. He is not to cast lustful glances at strange women, nor at the wives of relatives, friends, gurus, priests or kings. He should not look upon naked women should they belong to another. He should show hospitality and be kind and friendly towards all with whom he has dealings, including all servants. For all the deeds of all men are watched by the gods above, and bad deeds will always devour their perpetrators, just as the demon Rahu devours the moon at the eclipse. And

I will give you one more piece of advice: keep your desires under control as a turtle hides his limbs under his shell, for unbridled lust nurtures the danger of unpropitious deeds. You conceal in your body both mortality and immortality: if you remain a fool, you will die; if you find truth, you will become immortal. Nothing in the world is as perspicacious as knowledge, science and wisdom, nothing purges a man like the truth, nothing is so gratifying as generosity, and nothing enslaves like greed. He who has nothing, has no enemies. If you rid yourself of greed, you will achieve peace. The highest happiness you can achieve is knowledge. He who has knowledge has

more than anyone else, and that is the best thing of all. Material possessions weigh nothing, for they are transient. Anyone can take them away. What you know and what is known to you, no one can take away."

"Who is worthy of the greatest honour, Bhishma?" asked Yudhishthira again. "I could listen to you for ever, for your words are pearls of wisdom."

"The greatest honour," replied Bhishma, "is deserved by those who know the highest truths the universe can boast. They are those who study the writs, are restrained and disciplined, and are never proud, never tell lies and are kind and obliging."

"You have spoken beautifully and

wisely, Bhishma," said Vyasa. "But now allow us to return to the city."

"Go," said Bhishma softly, "but do not forget me. And you, Yudhishthira, drive all doubt out of your bosom, and become a good ruler."

They all bowed respectfully to Bhishma, hands joined at the height of their foreheads, and withdrew humbly. Bhishma only sighed.

Back in Hastinapura, Yudhishthira devoted himself mainly to affairs of state. He looked after the widows and orphans of all the brave warriors who had died in the great battle, dealt with all the legal disputes which were awaiting judgement, disbanded and rebuilt

his army, and gave presents to the poor and the holy men. His nobility, justice, perspicacity and prudent and proper dealings earned him the respect and love of the inhabitants of town and country, and even of the wild tribes of the mountains and forests.

When the spring equinox was close at hand, and the sun moved northwards again, Yudhishthira decided to visit Bhishma again. He went with a long procession of magnificent coaches, light chariots, war chariots and heavy waggons. At its head rode the standard-bearers, the trumpeters and drummers, and behind them in the place of honour the blind old King

Dhritarashtra and his wife Gandhari. After them came the Pandus, courtiers and noblemen, holy men and wise priests, singers, musicians and poets. Heavy buffalo waggons drew up the rear, laden with fragrant ointments and oils, flowers and garlands, silken cloths, jugs of ghee, and sandal and aloe wood, all in readiness for a funeral pyre.

When they reached Bhishma, still lying on his bed of arrows, Yudhishthira bowed to him respectfully and said: "I did not forget you, my great uncle. I have come to visit you, along with the rest. King Dhritarashtra is here, and Queen Gandhari; my brothers are here, as are Krishna, Vidura and Sanyjaya. Tell me, kind great uncle, what I am to do."

Bhishma took Yudhishthira by the hand and said in a firm, clear voice: "I am glad you are all here, Yudhishthira. I have lain on this bed of arrows for fifty-eight days. I suffered great pain, greater than I can describe, and yet I still did not want to die. But today I do not want to live any longer; I long to die, and so I will die. And all of you who have come here to visit me, remember that there is nothing higher than truth. Keep the truth, fight for truth, never betray the truth!"

Those were Bhishma's last words. He closed his eyes, concentrated his mind, and adjusted his breathing. All his wounds suddenly healed, and Bhishma died.

From the heavens came the lugubrious sound of divine tympani, and fresh, dew-laden flowers of all colours rained down on Bhishma's dead body.

Old Vidura and the Pandu brothers built a huge funeral pyre of fragrant woods. Then they dressed Bhishma's body in silk, laid it on the pyre, and rained flowers upon it. Yuyutsu held a white parasol above it, and Bhima and Arjuna fanned it with two white yaks' tails. Nakula and Sahadeva stood beside them and held the symbol of Bhishma's caste and dignity, his jewellery and arms. Yudhishthira and Dhritarashtra fanned the dead body with palm leaves.

The priests and holy men recited the sacred verses of the *Vedas*, and sang ceremonial hymns. The sacrificial priests dripped ghee on the sacred fire which they had lit a little way off, muttering the ancient *mantras*. Then they lit the funeral pyre.

Reconciliation

Soon afterwards Abhimanyu's widow, Uttara, gave birth to a son, but due to the effect of Ashwatthaman's fearful weapon, he was born dead. Krishna heard a loud wailing and mournful cries from the women's chambers, and hurried to see what was wrong. Half way there he met Kunti and Draupadi, in tears and on their way to ask him for help.

"Krishna, save little Parikshit if you can," wailed Kunti, Parikshit's great-grandmother. And the tearful Draupadi grabbed him by the sleeve and said: "Come, quickly; Uttara is in despair!"

Krishna hurried to the chamber of the unhappy mother and gave orders for a garland of white flowers to be brought, earthenware jugs filled to the brim with spring water, sandal wood and toasted mustard seed in ghee. He then lit the sacred fire in all corners of the room, and hung bright and shining weapons on the walls. In this way the room was freed of all evil spirits and powers. The red-eyed Uttara sat on her bed and with clasped hands gave honour to Krishna. Her face showed both bitter despair and a spark of the hope she placed in the noble Krishna.

Krishna went up to the largest jug of spring water, touched the surface of the water, and in a ceremonial voice called: "In return for all the good I have done, I ask for this child to be restored to life! As I have always honoured the god of the moral order, Dharma, and kept his commands and laws, I ask for this child to be returned to life! I ask for Parikshit, son of Abhimanyu, to live!"

Before he had even finished speaking, little Parikshit began to wave his arms and kick his legs, and to scream at the top of his voice. Krishna smiled, and all the women present were filled

with joy; only Uttara again began to cry, this time with immeasurable happiness. Parikshit was alive and well, and at once he began to suck hungrily at his mother's breast.

The house of Pandu had passed into a further generation.

The Pandus had ruled the whole kingdom for fifteen years, and they ruled justly and prudently, without excesses. There were no wars in the land, the harvests were abundant, the cattle and other domestic animals were plentiful, and it seemed as if thieving had died out. Old King Dhritarashtra and his wife Gandhari were honoured as if they had been the Pandus' own parents. Everyone knew the great sorrow suffered by the old king and queen, so they tried hard to make them happy, contented and without cares.

Only Bhima was sometimes unable to control his hatred for all Kurus, and he bribed the servants not to obey Dhritarashtra and Gandhari, not to carry out their orders. Gandhari did not really notice, but it grieved blind old Dhritarashtra greatly. He did not complain to Yudhishthira, which would have been beneath his dignity, but one day he said to Nakula and Sahadeva who were particularly kind to him: "The true cause of the doom of my hundred sons was my own foolishness. I did not consider wisely. I acted crazily when I made Duryodhana king. I was truly blind then, but after the great struggle I saw the light, blind though I am. For a long time I have been fasting, and I often dress in a deerskin and sleep on a simple bed made of holy grass. I devote myself to meditation and penitence, in order to cleanse my soul from sins and wrongdoing. It is time for me to make an important decision."

Nakula and Sahadeva took their leave of him politely, and left in a dilemma, not understanding what Dhritarashtra had in mind. But they said nothing to Yudhishthira.

In fact, Dhritarashtra himself told him.

When, one evening, Yudhishthira came as usual to wish the old king good night, Dhritarashtra told him: "Listen carefully, Yudhishthira. I have lived here with my wife happily and in plenty for the last fifteen years. But now I wish to ask you to allow me to leave for the quiet of the forests, and to spend the rest of my life in penitence and contrition. I am old, and do not belong at the royal court. You, too, will participate in my penitence, since the king is a part of all which goes on in his kingdom."

"Stay with us," Yudhishthira begged him, surprised. "Do not go away from here; you are king, and I only do as you decide, advise and suggest!"

"I cannot stay here any longer," Dhritarashtra said firmly. "I have decided after much consideration."

"A king once as strong as the leader of an elephant herd!" cried Yudhishthira. "A king who crushed an iron statue of Bhima in his embrace, and now as weak as a woman!"

"I am not weak in spirit," said King Dhritarashtra. "Only my body is wilting and dying. Therefore I wish to leave, as befits an old man."

"Do not keep him here," the wise Vidura told Yudhishthira. "His decision is the right one. He is old, and has no sons. His life is reaching its end."

Yudhishthira clasped his hands at forehead height and said to Vidura: "I honour you as I honour my own father, since you are our guru. I will not keep Dhritarashtra here."

Then King Dhritarashtra and his royal spouse Gandhari made the necessary preparations for their departure and undertook the proper ceremonies. The next morning old Vidura went to Yudhishthira in the throne-room and told him that Dhritarashtra and Gandhari would leave on the night of the first autumn full moon, but that he asked for enough gold pieces to hold a last ceremony in memory of his hundred fallen sons and of Bhishma and Drona.

Bhima burst out angrily: "What need has he of more money? Ceremonies have already been held. Why should we go to so much trouble over those who sent us into exile? And Dhritarashtra did not so much as lift a finger to stop them."

"You are my elder brother, Bhima," said Arjuna, "and I do not wish to oppose you, but do not allow your anger and hatred to get the better of you."

Yudhishthira turned to Vidura and smiled at him. "Tell Dhritarashtra he shall have all he asks," he told him. "Take no notice of Bhima's angry words; he does not really mean what he says."

Bhima just rolled his eyes, and was silent.

Then came the night of the first full moon of the autumn. Dhritarashtra and Gandhari, dressed only in simple white garments, left the royal palace. All the inhabitants of the capital city gathered along the main street, which was in those days called the royal way; they crowded to windows and balconies, and sadly took their leave of the old king and his dedicated wife.

Mother Kunti had decided she would go to the forest hermitage with them, but Yudhishthira tried to persuade her not to. "No, mother, not you!

Come back to the royal palace, and look after your daughters-in-law!"

Kunti, however, was not to be dissuaded; she took Queen Gandhari by the hand and set off resolutely out of the city. "I will live in the forest with you," she said. "I will do penance, and serve you as if you were my mother-in-law and father-in-law."

The Pandu brothers caught up with the trio as they were leaving, and Yudhishthira said urgently: "Mother, your decision is a strange one! Do not do this. We do not want you to go. How can you leave us all? Change your mind, I beg of you!"

When Kunti heard him, her eyes filled with tears. But she did not let go of Gandhari's hand, and walked steadfastly on.

Now Bhima, too, begged her: "Mother, dear mother, do not leave us! Do as Yudhishthira asks. We need you here!"

Kunti held back her grief, dried her eyes, and walked on. Then she said to her sons gravely and emphatically: "When you lost your kingdom, I tried to encourage you not to lose your heads and hearts as well. I always tried to give you courage in your hour of need, and to rid you of uncertainty, doubt and hesitation. Now you need me no longer. The great struggle has

long been over, and I know that the house of Pandu will not die out. Let me go; I know well enough what I am doing. Always be noble, and keep to the moral code."

And at last the Pandus understood their mother's decision.

All those who accompanied them went back to the royal city; only Yudhishthira, Vidura and Sanyjaya went with the three resolute penitents deep into the forest. There they helped them build a shelter and three beds from sacred grass. Then they took their leave of them.

Dhritarashtra, Gandhari and Kunti dressed in the manner of hermits, in deerskins, bast and bark, and began to live the life of forest penitents. They kept a tight rein on their desires, denied themselves their wishes, disciplined their minds, and tamed all their senses. They devoted themselves to contrition and meditation, and lived only off fruits and roots, drinking clear water from a spring. Soon they were all skin and bone, but their spirits were sharp, quick to understand, and perspicacious.

In the thirty-sixth year after the great battle, Yudhishthira saw many unsettling signs: hot sandstorms drove through the city, birds flew backwards, rivers flowed upstream and uphill, a thick fog rolled constantly along the horizon; stars fell from the heavens, the sun was engulfed in darkness,

headless bodies appeared at twilight, swaying to and fro, and around the sun and the moon blood-red clouds gathered. These were signs of evil days.

That year the Yaduan royal city was visited by three divine priests, Vishwamitra, Kanva and Narada. Krishna's wicked and malicious son Shamba dressed as a woman, painted his face and bedecked himself with jewels, and, in order to make fun of the holy men, his companions introduced him thus: "This is the wife of the respected citizen Bahbru; she is with child, and would like to have a son. Tell us, holy priests, what sort of a son will be born to her? What qualities and talents will he have?"

The holy men did not fall for this ruse, and replied sternly: "Shamba will indeed give birth; he shall give birth to an iron club, which will spell the doom of the whole house of the Yaduas. For you Yaduas have become too proud; self-esteem has turned your heads, and so you will not escape punishment. You will destroy yourselves; you will kill each other. Only Krishna and his brother Balarama will escape death in that battle, but afterwards Balarama will be swallowed by the ocean, and Krishna will be slain by the hunter, Jara."

Then the holy priests went to see Krishna, and repeated this prophecy to him. Krishna paid his respects to them, as befitted, and the priests left Dwaraka. Krishna shut himself in his chambers and devoted himself to meditation, for he knew the prophecy of the holy priests to be inexorable.

The next day Shamba gave birth to a huge iron club. All were horrified, for they knew that the dreaded prophecy was being fulfilled. The Yaduan king, Ugrasena, at once gave orders for the club to be ground to dust and the dust thrown into the sea. At the same time he ordered a ban on the manufacture and sale of alcoholic drinks, under punishment of impalement on a stake. But this did not prevent the prophecy from coming true.

The terrible lord of time, Kala, came rushing into the city of Dwaraka; he had bronzed skin, a bald head and a piercing stare, which sought out everything. Rats and mice ran about the streets and forced their way into houses, shops and stores. They ate everything they came across, and nibbled at the fingernails and ear-lobes of those who slept. Earthenware jugs and pots cracked open of their own accord. Goats howled desperately like jackals, cows gave birth to donkeys, and bitches had kittens.

But the Yaduans took no notice of these unpropitious omens, and behaved in a wanton, rude and shameless manner, as if they were possessed by a desire to bring about their own doom. Insults to gods, Brahmans and ancestors were a common occurrence, and not even gurus and parents were spared. Men and women gave themselves over to adultery and fornication. Blazing fires threw shadows to the left-hand side. Freshly-prepared dishes, just brought from the kitchen, were suddenly full of wriggling worms the moment they were set before the diners. And there were also ill omens to be seen on the moon.

The women of Yadua had nightmares about a black, disembowelled witch with white fangs, who laughed wildly and lurked the streets of Dwaraka tearing the holy cords from their wrists. The men of Yadua dreamed of vile, moulting vultures who ate their innards, liver, heart, spleen and kidneys, and pulled out knotted intestines and inflated stomachs. But in the morning they always forgot these dreams, and set out at once in search of pleasure and vice. Nor did anyone any longer take any notice of the king's prohibition of alcoholic drinks.

One day the Yaduans and their friends organised a merry trip to Prabhasa. The best foods, which should have been given to the Brahmans, were urinated on in a drunken revel, and thrown to the apes. The musicians played for all they were worth, and the singers shouted each other down. And all ate and drank to their hearts' content. It was a lively feast, but destined to end tragically.

Satyaki, Krishna's charioteer, at-

tacked Kritavarman, who had been on the side of the Kurus at the great battle, and insulted him publicly. "What sort of Kshatriya kills unarmed warriors in their sleep?" he taunted. "Clear off! We don't want anything to do with you!"

Kritavarman made a very rude gesture with his left hand, and retorted: "What about you? You killed Bhurishravas while he was lost in meditation!"

Satyaki shouted: "I'll kill you, as you and Ashwatthaman killed the sleeping sons of Draupadi!" And he leapt upon him. With a single blow of his sword he cut off his head, and then struck out on all sides like a madman.

The Bhojas and Andhakas quickly finished the wine in their cups, and then used the cups to beat Satyaki to death. Krishna's son Pradyumna, whom Krishna begot with Rukmini, daughter of the King of Vidharbha, ran to Satyaki's aid, but he was beaten to death, too.

Even Krishna was carried away by the general fury. He grasped handfuls of the grass that grew nearby in large tufts, and each blade turned into a huge club, reminiscent of the club which Shamba had given birth to shortly before. Krishna threw these clubs into the mêlée of tussling men, killing several of them. But the others grabbed hold of the clubs, and the merciless carnage continued, and even grew in ferocity.

Krishna sent the charioteer Daruka to Arjuna to tell him that the Yaduans had unleashed their own doom, and were killing each other. Then he said to Balarama: "Wait for me here. I will lead the women and children to safety."

In the capital city, Dwaraka, he put the women and children under the protection of his father, Vasudeva, telling him: "Look after them until Arjuna comes. I must return to Balarama." He respectfully touched his father's feet with his forehead, and started to leave.

The women and children began to weep, and they were inconsolable.

"Do not worry," Krishna comforted them. "Arjuna will soon be here, and he will protect you."

When Krishna returned to Balarama, he found him sitting in the lotus position, lost in yoga meditation. Slowly, very slowly, a huge, thousand-headed snake with eyes as red as rubies was crawling out of his mouth. It crawled into the waves of the ocean, and then the ocean rolled forward and swallowed Balarama up. Thus ended Balarama's pilgrimage through this world.

Krishna knew very well that fate is inexorable, but his brother's death affected his spirit deeply. He went into the forest and, recalling the curse of Queen Gandhari, took up the lotus position and fell into meditation. The hunter Jara happened to be passing that way, and he supposed he saw a deer. He shot an arrow with a twice-tempered point, and hurried to pick up his booty. But instead of a deer he saw a calmly seated yogi with many arms, dressed in a sacred orange robe. The horrified hunter fell at the yogi's feet and begged his forgiveness. Krishna forgave him, for it was not the hunter's fault, and then he rose up to heaven, where to the singing and playing of the heavenly *gandharvas* he was welcomed by Indra himself.

When the charioteer Daruka told Arjuna the news of the murderous battle which was raging among the Yaduans, Arjuna took his leave of his brothers and drove with all speed to Dwaraka.

The city looked like a mourning widow. No sooner had Arjuna reached Krishna's palace, than he was embraced by the dejected Vasudeva, Krishna's father, who told him with tears in his eyes: "I, an old man, am still alive, but all the rest are dead!"

The wives of the slaughtered Yaduans and their children wept, moaned and lamented, most of all the sixteen thousand wives of Krishna.

Arjuna was seized with terrible grief, and said: "Without Krishna the world has lost its sheen; but I must take the women and children to Indraprastha, where they will be safe."

But before everything could be made ready, before the waggons and carts could be loaded and all could be assembled ready to leave, old Vasudeva peacefully passed away. And again a great lamentation arose in the royal palace of the city of Dwaraka.

Onto the funeral pyre of the dead Vasudeva stepped his four wives, Devaki, Bohemiadra, Rohini and Madira. Arjuna himself was in charge of the ceremony.

At last that long caravan of waggons, buffalo carts, horses, camels, elephants and people set off from the city. But no sooner had the long procession left the city walls, than a huge wave rose up from the ocean, full of sharks, crocodiles and other sea monsters, and in an instant washed away the whole of the once glorious royal city of the Yaduans, so that not one brick, not a beam or a tile remained.

The people in the caravan cried out: "What a terrible fate! Quickly, quickly! Hurry! We must escape! How terrible!" And the caravan went on its way with all speed, and no one even dared turn to look upon that spectacle.

One night, the caravan made camp in a pleasant grove on the banks of a gushing stream, and no one had any idea that the area was plagued with a gang of merciless robbers. Their chief ordered scouts to follow the caravan. Then he told his men: "There are only women and children there, and a single bowman. Take everything you can lay your hands on, and show no mercy!"

They attacked without warning, as when a mountain top is toppled by lightning, roaring like a whole pack of angry lions. Arjuna picked up his bow called *Gandiva* and said to himself: "You will regret your foolish deed, and will long remember this day. I will destroy you with my arrows."

But he was wrong. He could scarcely string his bow, and managed to fire only a few arrows. He tried in vain to use his divine weapons. Nothing went right for him. Suddenly, he was even short of arrows. What could be the matter? What had happened? Arjuna could not explain it, so he blamed the whole thing on fate.

The robbers took almost everything, and carried off the most beautiful of the women. Some of the uglier ones went of their own accord. What could Arjuna do?

With the handful of women who were left and the children and a few waggons, they reached Indraprastha. There Rukmini and others of Krishna's wives decided to end their own lives; they climbed onto a funeral pyre and had themselves burned, so that they

might go to meet their divine husband in heaven. Others, led by Satyabhama, went off into the deep forest and gave themselves over to penitence.

Arjuna set off all alone to visit the holy sage Vyasa in his forest hermitage. When he arrived, the holy man was deep in meditation, so he sat down quietly and waited. Afterwards he greeted Vyasa as was fitting, and paid his respects, for he was a true guru.

"Welcome, Arjuna," Vyasa said. "What has happened to you? Have you been splashed by some unclean water?"

"Krishna is dead," replied Arjuna. "All the Yaduans have killed each other. My heart is empty. What am I to do?"

And Vyasa replied: "It was a curse, and the curse has been fulfilled. Thus was it spoken, and so it had to be. There was no way out. Krishna could have prevented it, but after consideration he let it happen. So there is no reason to regret it. Behind all things, Arjuna, stands the mighty god of time, Kala. Kala gives, and Kala takes away; Kala distributes, and Kala attributes. Kala is the seed of the universe. And all things are constantly in motion; all things turn, all things change, all things pass, all things keep moving. There is no appeal against it, no help for it." Thus spoke the holy sage Vyasa.

Arjuna bowed silently to Vyasa with his hands clasped before his forehead,

and, deep in thought, hurried back to Hastinapura to tell Yudhishthira all that had happened.

The news of the destruction of the Yaduans prostrated the Pandus with grief. Without the noble Krishna the world had no meaning. Yudhishthira decided he would leave everything behind and live without a home.

"Time governs all things, in time all is created and destroyed," he said to Arjuna. "We are all victims of time."

"You are right, brother," replied Arjuna. "Nothing is of lasting value; all is transient. If you allow me, I will go with you."

The other brothers, Bhima, Nakula and Sahadeva, decided to do likewise, as did their communal wife, the lovely, black-eyed and dark-lashed Draupadi. Yudhishthira proclaimed little Parikshit king, and asked Dhritarashtra's noble bastard, Yuyutsu, to protect him and keep an eye on affairs of government.

He told Parikshit's mother, Uttara: "Your son is now king in Hastinapura. Do not abandon him, but support him, and make sure he does nothing which is against the moral order."

The Pandu brothers gave away all their jewellery, gold and precious stones, splendid garments, pedigree horses and fine chariots to the people and the Brahmans, took their leave of everyone, and left the royal city

dressed only in the simple garb of penitents. They looked just the same as
when, many years before, they had left
Hastinapura after their lost game of
backgammon. But today they were
happy, for they had taken a step in the
direction of eternal salvation, towards
breaking the bonds of earthly being.

At the head of the group strode
Yudhishthira, resolute in his decision.
Behind him came Bhima, then Arjuna,
and, according to age, Nakula and
Sahadeva; last of all came Draupadi,
their devoted wife, as befits a woman.
And behind them all walked a stray
dog which had appeared from somewhere or other.

They wandered for a long time,
crossing many lands, many countries;
they descended into valleys, and then
again climbed into the mountains; they
waded across rivers, and walked round
broad lakes. They went towards the
south east, and when they reached the
coast turned to the north-north-west,
then to the west. In this manner they
reached the spot where the Yaduan
capital Dwaraka had once stood, before it was swallowed by the ocean.

Then they headed north-north-east,
to the immeasurably great Himalayan
mountains. They paid no heed to the
tribulations of their arduous trek, but
crossed the mountain range through
passes where footpaths led, until they
reached a broad, sandy plateau. In
the distance they could see the slim

outline of the sacred mountain Meru.

The resolve of the Pandu brothers and their wife Draupadi was unshaken. They crossed the sandy plain and began to climb the steep slopes of Mount Meru. But Draupadi slipped, and went hurtling down among the rocky crevices below.

"No one has done any wrong," said Bhima. "Then why did she die?"

"We all loved her with the same love," said Yudhishthira. "But she loved Arjuna most of all. Now she has paid the price."

The Pandu brothers climbed higher and higher. Then Sahadeva's foot slipped, and he fell into the precipice.

Bhima said: "Sahadeva was always modest and respectful, and did nothing against the moral order. Why, then, did he fall?"

"He thought," replied Yudhishthira, "that he was the cleverest of all. Now he has paid the price."

And the brothers climbed on, the dog still following them. Then Nakula fell.

"Our brother Nakula was most righteous and obedient. Why did he have to die?" asked Bhima.

And Yudhishthira replied: "He was righteous and obedient, and always behaved properly. But he supposed he was the handsomest of us all. Now he has paid the price, for every man must accept his own fate. There is no way out."

Arjuna was deeply affected by the loss of the beautiful Draupadi and his two younger brothers. His eyes were filled with tears, and he missed his footing; losing his grip on a root to which he was holding, and he in his turn went hurtling down to the foot of the holy mountain.

Bhima looked down after him, and said: "Arjuna never lied, not even in jest. What did he do wrong, that he had to die?"

And Yudhishthira replied: "Arjuna vowed he would kill all his enemies in a single day. He was a proud and bold warrior, but he did not keep his word. Now he has paid the price."

And the two brothers climbed on, struggling towards the peak of the sacred Mount Meru. The stray dog followed them, its tongue hanging out.

Suddenly Bhima cried out: "I am falling! I always loved you with a sincere brotherly love. Why am I falling?"

"You were too boastful, and ate too much, not heeding the needs of others. Now you are paying the price," Yudhishthira called after him, and he climbed on, and on. The dog was still at his heels.

When Yudhishthira and the dog had dragged themselves up to the summit of Mount Meru, the heavens and the earth shook with thunder, and the god Indra himself appeared in his flying chariot. "Come, Yudhishthira," he said

warmly. "Step into my chariot, and come with me into paradise."

"Thank you, O mighty god Indra, but wherever I go, there shall my brothers and our common wife go too. And they have fallen to the foot of the holy mountain."

"You will meet them in paradise," said Indra. "They are there already, have no fear. *You* will enter paradise alive."

"What about this stray dog?" asked Yudhishthira. "He has followed me faithfully since we left Hastinapura. I have taken a liking to him. I cannot leave him here just like that."

"Yudhishthira," said Indra, impatiently, "you have just achieved final salvation, immortality and heavenly bliss. Forget the dog; leave him be."

"But the dog is faithful to me," Yudhishthira objected firmly. "I will not accept anything which means I must reject my friends!"

"There is no place in paradise for dogs, Yudhishthira! Leave him be, and you will do no wrong."

"No! This dog has given me his trust, his friendship. He needs me. I will not abandon him; that would be treacherous."

"Do not say so," said Indra. "You abandoned your wife Draupadi, and you abandoned your brothers. Why are you so concerned about a stray dog?"

"Draupadi and my brothers died," replied Yudhishthira, "and it was not in my power to bring them back to life. Therefore I left them where they had fallen. But this dog is alive, and he will not leave me. So I will not leave him, whatever the cost."

Then a strange thing happened: the mangy stray dog suddenly disappeared, and in its place stood the god of the moral order, Dharma.

"You are good, wise and noble," the god Dharma told Yudhishthira. "You are like your father, Pandu. You have again proved that you have sympathy for all creatures. No one is your equal in this. Therefore you may step into Indra's chariot without more ado; I will go with you, for the stray dog was I."

And Indra's flying chariot soared from the summit of the sacred mountain, Meru, and headed straight for paradise.

In Indra's paradise Yudhishthira was greeted by the divine priest, Narada, who addressed him thus: "Your

glory and nobility, Yudhishthira, exceed that of all the divine priests; therefore have you been admitted to paradise alive, in your earthly form. Live here in happiness."

"I cannot live happily," Yudhishthira objected, "until I am reunited with my brothers and our wife Draupadi. Without them this place of bliss is for me a place of grief."

"You are still affected by human feelings and emotions," Indra told him. "You still have a human body, so you cannot meet your brothers or Draupadi, who have already lost theirs. Here you should mix with the divine priests and with those who for their merits were also admitted to paradise in their bodily form."

"No! I cannot agree to that," cried Yudhishthira, indignantly. "I want to go where my brothers and our wife Draupadi are!"

"Calm yourself, Yudhishthira," the divine priest Narada reassured him. "Come, I will show you round Indra's paradise, and you will see for yourself."

He took Yudhishthira by the arm and led him away.

The first person Yudhishthira saw in Indra's paradise was Duryodhana, sitting proudly on a splendid throne and beaming with satisfaction.

A sudden wave of anger swept through Yudhishthira; he turned round, and in a loud voice said: "I do not in the least fancy sharing paradise with the niggardly and loutish Duryodhana. He treated us in the worst possible way; he was constantly dreaming up all sorts of plots against us, and he was the main cause of the great fratricidal struggle. I do not want to see him! I want to go where my brothers and Draupadi are."

The divine priest Narada smiled cordially and understandingly, and said: "My dear king, here in heaven the ties which bound you on earth are of no consequence; there is no hatred, and no enmity. Here in Indra's paradise Duryodhana's followers worship him as a god. Duryodhana sacrificed his body in the great struggle, and that is just as worthy a deed as if he had sacrificed it in the sacred fire. It is true that on earth he persecuted you and did evil by you, but on account of deeds worthy of a Kshatriya warrior he has been raised to heaven. Yudhishthira, forget the wrongs and the shame, the insults and humiliation you have suffered; forget the horrors of the great struggle. Now you are in paradise, and you should greet Duryodhana with dignity and courtesy. Hatred is over, bitter memories are gone!"

Yudhishthira was incensed by these words, and he burst out: "If paradise is a fitting place of refuge for a shameless murderer of friends and relatives, who goaded us into desperate vengeance, then show me, divine Narada, where my honourable and good brothers are! Where is Dhritarashtra? Where are Virata, Drupada, Shikhandin, Draupadi's sons, and Abhimanyu? And where is our wife, Draupadi? Take me away from here; this is not paradise. Paradise is where my brothers are."

At that the voices of the eternal gods could be heard, addressing Yudhishthira in chorus: "Dear son, if you wish to go where your brothers are, the heavenly guide is on his way. He will lead you where you wish to go."

In an instant the heavenly guide appeared before Yudhishthira. He shone like the drops of morning dew on blades of grass at dawn. "Come with me, O king," he said, with a respectful bow, and set off in a direction out of the heavenly glow and into misty darkness. Yudhishthira followed him, looking forward to meeting his brothers and Draupadi.

The way was a difficult, tortuous one. Instead of grass and herbs, it was overgrown with hair and beards. There were various unpleasant smells everywhere, and all were foul and clinging. Yudhishthira trudged along a path spattered with decaying blood, tripped over scattered bones, and waded through a quagmire of bone marrow and lymph. Through this foul stuff repulsive white and pink worms and fat larvae crawled. Over decomposing bodies clouds of black flies with silver wings and golden green blowflies with hairy legs buzzed to and fro, and rooks and vultures feasted on their entrails. All around evil spirits rushed, and demons and imps danced and cried.

The victorious King Yudhishthira clenched his teeth and walked on behind the glowing heavenly guide. He crossed a river of boiling, decaying water, pushed his way through a forest whose trees had blades instead of leaves, ran over a desert of burning sands, and swam across a lake of hot oil.

"How much further is it?" he asked the heavenly guide. "Is this also part of Indra's paradise?"

"This is the end of our journey," the heavenly guide replied. "We can go no further. We have no choice but to return, O king."

The stench became unbearable, and was more choking than ever. Yudhishthira, confused, exhausted and disappointed, turned to make his way back again.

Out of the darkness on either side came a desperate wailing from many throats: "Son of Pandu! Pandu! Take pity on us! Stay here, do not go away. Your presence is a fresh breeze, the sweet scent of woodland flowers! You have brought us great relief. We have seen you, and we are happy. Son of Kunti, do not go away, for while you are here our pain is not so great."

Yudhishthira's noble heart was filled

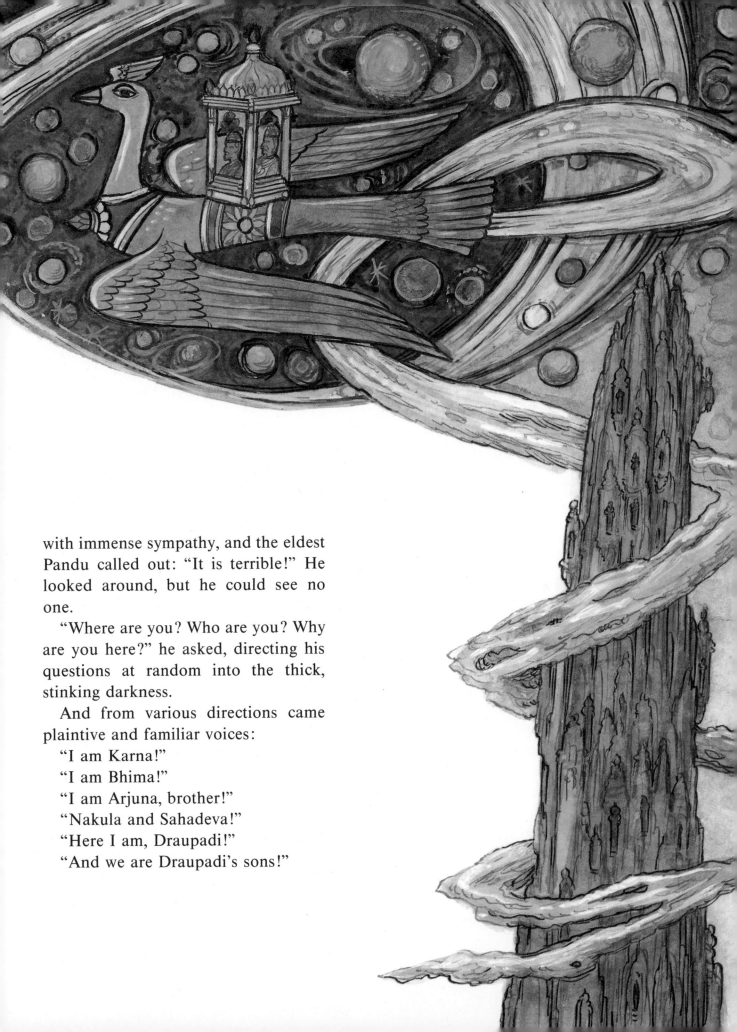

with immense sympathy, and the eldest Pandu called out: "It is terrible!" He looked around, but he could see no one.

"Where are you? Who are you? Why are you here?" he asked, directing his questions at random into the thick, stinking darkness.

And from various directions came plaintive and familiar voices:

"I am Karna!"

"I am Bhima!"

"I am Arjuna, brother!"

"Nakula and Sahadeva!"

"Here I am, Draupadi!"

"And we are Draupadi's sons!"

Yudhishthira was close to despair, and in his heart he lamented, wondering: "What terrible thing have they all done, that they should be consigned to this repulsive corner of Indra's paradise? What did Duryodhana do so nobly, that he sits on a splendid throne, looking so smug? Am I dreaming, or am I awake? Have I lost my senses? Or am I imagining all this?"

He cursed all the gods in heaven, including Indra and Dharma. Then he turned to the heavenly guide and told him: "Go! Go back to those who sent you, and tell them I will stay here, for my presence brings comfort to these poor souls condemned to spend their days in this dreadful corner of Indra's paradise."

Without a word, the heavenly guide disappeared, and at that instant Indra, king of the gods, appeared before Yudhishthira, in the company of Dharma and the other gods. The moment they arrived, a fragrant breeze drove away the repulsive stench, the darkness was dispelled, a heavenly glow shone all around, and the air was filled with the sweet smell of lotus blossoms.

Indra, king of the gods, smiled at Yudhishthira and said: "Yudhishthira, come closer, and lay aside your sorrow; do not feel wronged any longer. For the illusion, the spectre, is gone. You have stood the test, and have accounted yourself as befits a nobleman of the Kshatriya caste. The existence of all men is a mixture of good and evil. The bitter comes with the sweet, the unpleasant with the pleasant. And whoever tastes one, must also taste the other. Therefore we first sent you here, to get a taste of hell. But now you and your brothers, with your wife Draupadi and the rest of your kinsfolk, will enjoy all the delights of my paradise. The *gandharvas* will play and sing for you, and the heavenly nymphs, the *apsarasas,* will dance for you. Come and wash yourself in the heavenly River Ganges — in this way you will become a denizen of heaven. Your spirit will be cleansed, and your mind will be soothed. You will never again suffer unpleasant feelings or disturbing sensations."

Yudhishthira's heavenly father Dharma embraced his dear and good son, and said to him kindly: "My son, I tested you three times, and you pleased me each time. You are a paragon of our ancient moral order. The first test was your endurance of exile in the forest of Dwaitavana. For a second time I tested you when I accompanied you as a mangy stray dog. And a third time you proved your pure nature when you decided to stay in this stinking hell, in order to be with your brothers, Draupadi and the relatives and friends whom you did not wish to leave in such dire straits. I tell you, Yudhishthira, that none of your kin will be left in hell. It was all just an

illusion, created to test you for the last time. And you have stood the test well."

Indra, king of the gods, said: "Come back to my paradise, all of you. I invite you all warmly, and you will be my dearest guests for eternity."

And so the Pandu brothers, with their wife Draupadi, her sons and all the other kinsfolk, friends and followers left that repulsive hell and entered Indra's heaven. The inhabitants of heaven welcomed them joyously, and greeted them all. The Pandus gaily embraced old friends and long-lost relatives, and they bowed to their father Pandu and their mothers, Kunti and Madri, old King Dhritarashtra and his wife Gandhari, and Bhishma, Vidura and Drona.

It was a happy reunion of those who loved each other, and who had lived together through years of good and evil;

all this linked them with a firm bond which could not be broken, the eternal bond of shared existence, thoughts and action. That is something which cannot be replaced. It is the most precious of treasures, for it is not material, and thus does not decay or tarnish, and it brings a spiritual pleasure which is beyond compare in the whole universe.

In Vyasa's words there is
Much wisdom to be found;
But a fool would not learn,
If he read it a hundred times.
It is a tale of victory
In a great and cruel battle,
About which all should know,
Kings and vassals,
Pupils, teachers, holy men,
Artisans and merchants,
Herdsmen and farmers,
Girls, maidens and women,

Young, pregnant and old.
It is a great tale,
Full of excitement and action,
A tale of life's course.
I call to you! Hear me!
The moral order brings bliss.
Why do you not obey it?
Revels are not for ever,

Nor is want, tribulation or pain;
Only the moral order is eternal.
Never go against it,
Neither out of fear nor lust,
Nor foolishness nor rancour,
Nor love nor anger.
Only the moral order is for ever;
Along with your eternal souls.

Afterword

Epic poetry is a typical form in early Indian literature. The Vedas and other old religious and philosophical texts are full of it. It was customary on solemn occasions for singers to recite, to musical accompaniment, ancient legends — especially when the great horse sacrifice (the Ashvamedha) was in progress, or at funerals. Back in the middle of the 7th century BC the Chhandogyopanishada mentions a "fifth Veda", said to consist of the Puranas and the Itihases; later the fifth Veda was itself called Mahabharata. This was undoubtedly the historical fabric on which the oldest of the Indian epics, the famous Mahabharata and Ramayana, were embroidered. The events on which the Mahabharata is based appear to date from the end of the Rig veda period (the second half of the second millennium BC), and the heroes are the ancestors of King Parikshit and his son Janamejaya, whom later Vedic texts refer to as a contemporary. The Vedas also frequently mention the Bharata and Kuru dynasties. The name Mahabharata means literally "Great Epic of the Struggle between the Bharatas".

According to Indian tradition, the author of the Mahabharata was Krishna Dwaipayana, the Islander, son of a fisherman's daughter, Satyavati, and the holy man Parshara; he was later known as Vyasa. But the extent and the content of the epic indicate that it could not have been written by one person. The name Vyasa is a mere attribute, meaning "compiler, editor". The Vyasa was the leading figure among a group of learned men whose task it was to put in order the history of the world as the Indians knew it in those days. The Puranas, the events of the distant past, were entrusted to the Vyasa's pupil Lemaharshana, while he himself assumed responsibility for contemporary history. The most important event of the age was a great civil war which affected to a greater or lesser extent all the lands of northern India, the struggle between the Pandus and the Kurus. It is said that the core of the Mahabharata epic was dictated by the Vyasa to the god Ganesh, who agreed to act as his scribe. This original form of the Mahabharata is known as the Jaya, or "Victory", and it must have come into being immediately after the great struggle.

At the time the role of historians was played by singers, or bards. They were for the most part Bandinas, Magadhas and Sutas. Bandinas dealt with contemporary events and Magadhas recorded the royal family tree and dealt with the history of the king's ancestors, while Sutas (literally "charioteers") took the material collected by the two other groups and made it into unified wholes, which they recited at gatherings for the great sacrifices (yajna). Of higher rank than these three groups of historians were the Sanhitakaras, the creators of writings, great holy men and sages (such as Vyasa, Valmiki, etc.) who worked on the material put together by the Bandinas, the Magadhas and the Sutas, using it to make regular additions to the Puranas, right up to the Gupta dynasty, the golden age in the 4th—5th centuries AD. Some episodes were recited by wandering Kushilavas (who later developed into theatrical actors) and Pathakas (reciters), and later by Dharakas, who translated the classical narratives into the popular tongues (the Prâkrit). It can be seen that the epic texts were constantly being reworked over a long period of time, and that they owed their form to many different artists who revised and supplemented them.

It should be remembered that the holy Vedic texts, the shruts (literally "hearings", in the sense of something revealed to the ears by divine will), were closed, canonised texts. They could not be altered or added to, while other texts, the smrits (literally "remembrances") were constantly updated right into the Middle Ages; this applied particularly to all the Puranas, including the Mahabharata. One may suppose that the final version of the Mahabharata as it has come down to us dates from just before the time of Christ, when the oral tradition (passing on of texts "from the mouth to the ear", from teacher to pupil) slowly gave way to a written one, though various types of writing had been known in India prior to that.

The Mahabharata is one of the longest epics in the world. If one were to translate the whole of it, it would fill a score of books like this one.

Glossary

Apsaras

A mythical being, half goddess, half woman. The *apsaras* are water nymphs, usually the wives of gandharvas, and often the lovers of mortals. They are typified by their association with water and trees.

Ashwamedha

The great horse sacrifice — performed by kings to confirm their sovereignty and to expand their territory with the favour and protection of the gods. The sacrificial horse was allowed to roam freely for a whole year, tracked by a group of warriors. If it wandered into the territory of another king, he either had to go to war or be voluntarily subjected. After the year was up, the horse and other sacrificial animals were ceremonially slaughtered and offered to the gods in the sovereign's honour.

The "twice-born"

Members of the three highest castes, i.e. the Brahmans, the Kshatriyas and the Vaishyas. Their second "birth" was a ceremony at which a priest hung a sacred cord across the left shoulder and right side.

Vasus

A particular class of gods whose number is usually eight.

Ghee

A sort of Indian butter. Ghee is made from cow or buffalo milk by boiling it gently with constant stirring, and skimming the butter off the surface.

Guru

A spiritual teacher who taught the "twice-born" the *Vedas* and other religious and scientific texts. A true guru also influenced his pupils by good example and by his strength of personality.

Gandharva

A mythical being. The *gandharvas* are the spirits of the clouds, mists and waters, and were invoked at wedding ceremonies. They are the heavenly singers and musicians.

Itihasas (iti ha asa — "how it really was")

Texts dealing with recent, almost contemporary, history. Among these in Vyasa's days was the *Mahabharata,* though with the passing of time it became one of the *Puranas.*

Yaksa

A mythical supernatural being. The *yaksas* are the spirits of Mother Earth, guardians of the riches of the god Kuvera, which are hidden in the Earth.

Mantra

A sacred charm capable of fulfilling some wish.

The Puranas

Ancient tales, a collection of partly mythological and partly historical writings, a sort of exhaustive encyclopedia of hinduism and ancient history.

The Rajasuya

A great sacrifice to the gods together with a great banquet and distribution of gifts, mainly to the Brahmans and to subjected rulers. The *Rajasuya* was held by a sovereign ruler on the occasion of his aspergation (the Indians sprinkled water from the sacred rivers on their kings in the same way that European kings were anointed), thus confirming his sovereignty.

Rakshasa

A mythical demonic being. The *rakshasas* are the demons of the night; they eat meat, partly human flesh. They are found at burial grounds and like to disrupt sacrifices to the gods. They are hostile to humans.

The Aims of Existence

The lives of the ancient Indians had three guiding principles. *Dharma* (the moral order) is the sum of all religious and secular duties regarding sanctity, legality and generally accepted morals. *Artha* (profit) means material prosperity and success in social and financial affairs. *Kama* (delight) is that which satisfies physical and spiritual needs and cravings. It was only later that a fourth goal, *Moksa* (salvation) was added; in fact, it is merely another aspect of *Dharma*.

The Castes

There were four of them in ancient India. The highest was that of the Brahmans, the priests and spiritual intellectuals. The Kshatriyas were warriors, aristocrats and secular rulers. The Vaishyas were craftsmen, traders, healers and entrepreneurs in general. The Shudras were labourers, peasant farmers, journeymen — in short, the dependent working class. Those without a caste were the "untouchables", the outcasts.

The Upanishads

Literally "sitting near" — of pupil and teacher. Texts containing mainly philosophical matters, dating from the most recent Vedic period.

The Vedic texts ("Vedas")

The oldest documents in ancient Indian literature, chiefly religious philosophical verse. They appear to date from soon after the middle of the third millennium BC. They are not a unified work of literature, but comprise collections of hymns, poems, odes and prose passages, all of which were of practical significance and were used regularly in the religious life of the ancient Indians. For many centuries the *Vedas* were part of the oral tradition, like all other ancient Indian literature, and were only written down much later, long after the Indians began to use writing. The oldest gods of the *Vedas* are deified natural forces and phenomena, such as the sky-god Jaush, the fire-god Agni, the sun-god Surya, the earth-goddess Prithivi, the wind-god Vaju and the water-god Varuna. Vishnu and Shiva, later to be mighty deities, are still minor gods in the *Vedas*.

PANDUS, KURUS AND JADUS

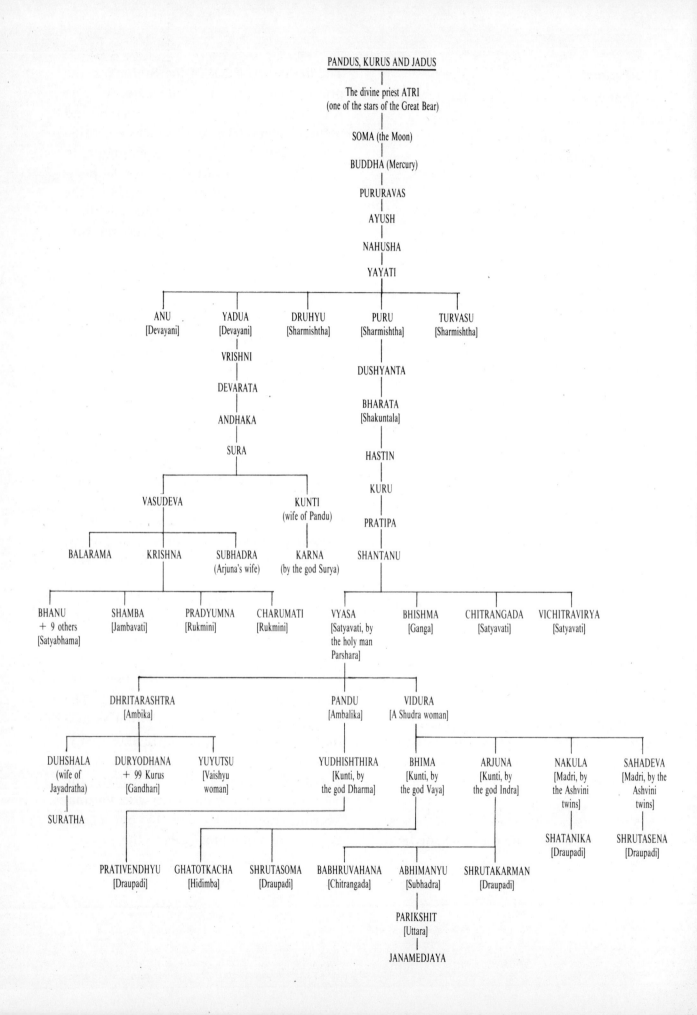

The divine priest ATRI
(one of the stars of the Great Bear)

SOMA (the Moon)

BUDDHA (Mercury)

PURURAVAS

AYUSH

NAHUSHA

YAYATI

ANU
[Devayani]

YADUA
[Devayani]

DRUHYU
[Sharmishtha]

PURU
[Sharmishtha]

TURVASU
[Sharmishtha]

VRISHNI

DEVARATA

ANDHAKA

SURA

DUSHYANTA

BHARATA
[Shakuntala]

HASTIN

KURU

PRATIPA

VASUDEVA

KUNTI
(wife of Pandu)

SHANTANU

BALARAMA

KRISHNA

SUBHADRA
(Arjuna's wife)

KARNA
(by the god Surya)

BHANU
+ 9 others
[Satyabhama]

SHAMBA
[Jambavati]

PRADYUMNA
[Rukmini]

CHARUMATI
[Rukmini]

VYASA
[Satyavati, by
the holy man
Parshara]

BHISHMA
[Ganga]

CHITRANGADA
[Satyavati]

VICHITRAVIRYA
[Satyavati]

DHRITARASHTRA
[Ambika]

PANDU
[Ambalika]

VIDURA
[A Shudra woman]

DUHSHALA
(wife of
Jayadratha)

DURYODHANA
+ 99 Kurus
[Gandhari]

YUYUTSU
[Vaishyu
woman]

YUDHISHTHIRA
[Kunti, by
the god Dharma]

BHIMA
[Kunti, by
the god Vaya]

ARJUNA
[Kunti, by
the god Indra]

NAKULA
[Madri, by
the Ashvini
twins]

SAHADEVA
[Madri, by the
Ashvini
twins]

SURATHA

SHATANIKA
[Draupadi]

SHRUTASENA
[Draupadi]

PRATIVENDHYU
[Draupadi]

GHATOTKACHA
[Hidimba]

SHRUTASOMA
[Draupadi]

BABHRUVAHANA
[Chitrangada]

ABHIMANYU
[Subhadra]

SHRUTAKARMAN
[Draupadi]

PARIKSHIT
[Uttara]

JANAMEDJAYA